The Derbyshire Set – Book 5

Regency Historical Romance

Arietta Richmond

Dreamstone Publishing © 2016

www.dreamstonepublishing.com

ISBN: 1925165671

ISBN-13: 978-1-925165-67-8

Books by Arietta Richmond

His Majesty's Hounds

Claiming the Heart of a Duke

Intriguing the Viscount

Giving a Heart of Lace (a prequel to Winning the Merchant Earl)

Being Lady Harriet's Hero

Enchanting the Duke (coming soon)

Redeeming the Marquess (coming soon)

Healing Lord Barton (coming soon)

Winning the Merchant Earl (coming soon)

Loving the Bitter Baron (coming soon)

Rescuing the Countess (coming soon)

Attracting the Spymaster (coming soon)

The Derbyshire Set

A Gift of Love (Prequel short story)

A Devil's Bargain (Prequel short story - coming soon)

The Earl's Unexpected Bride

The Captain's Compromised Heiress

The Viscount's Unsuitable Affair

The Count's Impetuous Seduction

The Rake's Unlikely Redemption

The Marquess' Scandalous Mistress

A Remembered Face (Bonus short story – coming soon)

The Marchioness' Second Chance (coming soon)

A Viscount's Reluctant Passion (coming soon)

Lady Theodora's Christmas Wish

The Duke's Improper Love (coming soon)

Other Books

The Scottish Governess (coming soon)

The Earl's Reluctant Fiancée (coming soon)

The Crew of the Seadragon's Soul Series, (coming soon - a set of 10 linked novels)

ARIETTA RICHMOND

For everyone who had the grace to be patient while this book, and the ones before and after it, were coming into existence, who provided cups of tea, and food, when the writing would not let me go, and endured countless times being asked for opinions.

For the readers coming to know these characters well, and who inspire me to continue, by buying my books!

And for all the writers of Regency Historical Romance, whose books I read, who inspired me to write in this fascinating period.

Chapter One

The glass slipped through his fingers, clipped the polished timber arm of the chair, and shattered. Whisky splashed - onto his elegant trousers, and his priceless Chinese rug. He cursed, half-heartedly, then simply sat there, brooding darkly.

Drinking didn't ease the pain and James Blackwood knew this. This did not stop him however, and had not stopped him once during the past eleven years of hard living. Really there was nothing at all that did seem to ease the pain, but he carried on, drinking and smoking, and gambling and womanizing, travelling the world, hunting and hosting the orgiastic parties for which he had become notorious.

To any outside observer it might have seemed like a fascinating existence, exciting, glamorous even, a life defined by freedom and adventure.

To Blackwood himself though, it had become boring, outstandingly dull, dry, a routine, and also a burden. He dragged an awful reputation with him and attracted the wrong sorts of people.

Where once he had enjoyed the dark and dangerous reputation that he had created, and the horrified, yet fascinated responses that it aroused in women, now it was tedious – he no longer wished to live up to the reputation that he had created for himself.

His manner of life had not made him happy for years, if indeed it ever had, and yet he carried on, seemingly unable to change even as it became more and more inappropriate and difficult as he got older.

He had drunk a lot in the past few months. Events at Amfield House he felt, had forced him to do so, or at least given him enough of an excuse that he was able to look at his ageing face in the mirror every morning and blame someone else.

He was still compellingly handsome, in a dark, mysterious way, and he knew this, though he was only thirty –two, he felt the press of old age slowly creeping in upon him and, in the back of his mind, he knew that his days as a serial seducer might soon be behind him.

Around the county balls and the marriage markets of high society, young ladies might be a little less concerned by a gentleman's age, looks, or virginal status than gentlemen were by those attributes in ladies, but this did not mean that any pretty young miss was willing to hitch up her petticoats for some old cad just because he had a twinkle in his eye and an intriguing reputation.

Like any other man about town, he had relied on his appearance at least as much as he had as on his aura of fascination and wry charm, his thick dark hair and gold flecked chestnut eyes that glistened in the candlelight, his firm jawline that shadows seemed to cling to, his penchant for the latest London fashions in dress.

If he carried on like this however, all that would fade away and he would be left an aging bachelor, with nothing, slowly drinking and gambling himself to death, unable to exert the sort of power he had once had over women, with only his servants and a dwindling circle of friends for company.

At least that was his fear, in the dark hours of the night, when he could not sleep, but had no distractions left to draw upon.

So many of Blackwood's friends had abandoned him over the years that he had lost count, and certainly he had lost any contact with most who might once have had a care for him. A few of course, he had rather actively fallen out with - Jenkinson had challenged him to a duel, only to flee to America at the last minute, to escape the possibility of an honourable death, and Manninghorn had retired to his obscure estate in Ireland, after Blackwood had positively run him out of town over gambling debts.

Many of them had married, and quit the rakish life of late-night carousing and whoring, which they had enjoyed (or at least, indulged in) with Blackwood. They had drifted away, to settle down to a life of domestic respectability, somewhere in the provinces. One such man, Henley, who had inherited a well-endowed Viscountcy, had even taken the trouble of writing a stern letter to him.

The self-righteous insistence presented in that letter, that Henley had enjoyed their companionship, but that they must never see each other again, now that he was living in rural Berkshire with a child on the way and a household to maintain, was rather galling, if also darkly amusing. Another, Denverton, had pulled Blackwood aside and threatened him with violence after he had felt that his former drinking associate was flirting rather too insistently with his fiancée. He was not wrong, Blackwood thought with a dark smile, although this abrupt termination of friendships brought him no joy now.

Around the great houses of England, James Blackwood's name was mostly disgraced, and few well-intentioned and respectable parents were naïve enough to let him anywhere near their daughters.

When you counted in those who had died- Illingford from a fever contracted in the West Indies, Newbury in a shipwreck in the Bay of Biscay, and even a number killed in the war, Blackwood had few he could call on for support. Three of those whom he could generally count on were here today, in his London townhouse, helping him to work his way through several bottles of whiskey, and at least as many again of Port.

There was Tomlinson, a tall and fresh-faced gentleman who did not look his thirty-four years, the youngest son of the Earl of Sussex. He had disgraced himself by having an affair with a chambermaid, been disinherited by his father, and now lived off a modest allowance and a few investments. Likewise Cranston, who had spent time in a Lancashire jail for duelling and now lived largely by gambling, spending wildly when he was in luck, leaning heavily on acquaintances when he was out of it.

And then there was Travers, Blackwood's protégé, a confirmed bachelor for life and a hard-living Marquess who spent about as much time on his country estate in Cornwall as he did on the surface of the moon. Over the years, Travers had frittered away most of his considerable fortune keeping up with Blackwood, running around London society seducing young ladies, holding lavish parties in his Mayfair townhouse, and betting hundreds of guineas on single horse races. Of all his friends, Travers was probably the closest, but they were ageing together with little dignity, and in both their cases the money was starting to run out.

This unfortunate financial situation had not, however, prevented the four of them from passing a raucous afternoon at Epsom racecourse for the annual Derby Stakes. It was one of the premier occasions of the London social calendar, a chance for well-bred (and not so well-bred!) young ladies and gentlemen to see and be seen, meet potential spouses and reinforce their place in high society. The young ladies had been radiant, the drink plentiful, and the horses as fast and daring as ever. It had been a perfect occasion for Blackwood and his companions.

"- Good god sir! That final furlong!" exclaimed Cranston, ignoring the broken glass and continuing as if nothing had happened, recalling memories of a few hours past. "... Damned if I've ever seen a runner come back like that! He was going like the clappers, incredible!"

"It would have been considerably more impressive..." said Travers, interjecting "... had any of us had the good sense to actually back the accursed horse. What was his name, Busby, or something?"

"Damned stupid name for a racehorse if ever I heard one" Cranston cut in "When was the last time you heard of a 50 to 1 outsider winning the Derby? When for that matter, was a 50 to 1 outsider even running in the Derby? I smell foul play, some rake has had us all for fools."

"Not that you ever seem to have the good sense to back the right horse, my good man" replied Travers. "I feel your case would be somewhat stronger if you had a record for managing anything but haemorrhaging guineas like you'd contracted a nasty fever and they were dropping out of your bowels"

"A charming image" said Tomlinson, sarcastically, smoking a fat cigar as he leant back in his chair with his feet resting on the table. "You're not quite as bad as Jimmy here though…"

Some of Blackwood's acquaintances called him Jimmy. It didn't yet annoy him quite enough for him to tell them to stop.

"- backs the wrong bloody horse all the damned time! Not just at the races mind!" the other three men laughed raucously.

Blackwood had the decency to smile, but tonight these jibes hurt more than usual. They had all heard by now about the situation at Amfield, how he had been rejected by Blanchette Cavendish and disgraced in a duel by a Captain of the Guards. It seemed that all of high society had heard something of the unfortunate affair, and his so-called friends were determined not to let any of it rest.

"What was her excuse this time, Jimmy old boy? Had to pop off to see her aunt about a lapdog? Or maybe sick of having one hanging around all the time and asking for someone to get rid of it!" they all laughed again, most pointedly at him.

If only they knew, he thought, about the seduction in the library, then they'd think twice before comparing him to a damned lapdog. He tried to muster a witty response but was too drunk, too tired, and, if truth be told, too depressed, to manage.

"I will remind you, Jeremiah Tomlinson, that you are a guest in my house, and I can just as soon have you ejected as have you sit here drinking my best whisky and resting your filthy boots on my table!"

"Oof, touched a nerve have we?" Tomlinson reacted sarcastically. "… cheer up Jim, not the end of the world! You only lost, what, forty guineas and all of your honour?" More laughter, and this time Blackwood felt it as a body blow. He could not stand it any longer, this inane, manly banter, this mockery of his honour. All he wanted was for these three imbeciles to leave him in peace.

"Forty, as opposed to your sixty-five, and at least I can afford it!" genuine anger strayed into his voice.

"Steady on old chap!" Tomlinson blurted in response. "What are you going to do? Challenge me to a duel and then miss wildly? I can tell you, I might not have the same sense of mercy as that blustering Captain! I might actually have to shoot you for that particular remark!"

Something snapped inside – James could feel it, almost a physical release of long dammed pressure. "Get out of my damned house you dog!" He could not contain himself "… if you want to speak to me like that, you can buy your own bloody drinks. Go!"

Drink had suppressed all inhibition and sorrow had stifled any wit or charm. He wanted nothing more than to wrap his hands around Tomlinson's neck and wring all life out of him, but he could not summon the energy. Instead, he hauled himself to his feet, a little unsteadily, but with as much dignity as he could muster, flung the door to his drawing room open, and gestured forcefully for them all to leave. Tomlinson and Cranston looked sheepish as they left, but Travers, to whom he was far closer, gave him a knowing wink, before skulking off with the other pair into the London night.

Blackwood sank into his chair, took another glass, poured himself more whisky, and lit up a cigarillo. As so often happened, when he was in low spirits and alone, his thoughts turned to Honour. *'What a strange sort of curse it is'* he thought to himself *'that my dear' lost love' shares her name with a virtue I shall never possess.'* There was a cynical edge to his thought, as he reminded himself, again, that in reality, she had been just as much of an uncaring, self-serving whore as most women were, when it came down to it. Whatever she had said to him when they were together, she had been quick enough to up and marry some old man with money.

It had all been such a cruel twist of fate. He had met her, his dream, his ideal, the woman who could have saved him from this messy and sordid existence, when he was too young, too shy, too foolish to take advantage. Honour had astounded him with her beauty, her wit, her bearing, her whole manner of assurance and grace, but it seemed that her words had been lies, that she had not shared his feelings, and she had gone off to marry some rich old man of whom her father approved.

Nothing had ever really gone Blackwood's way since, despite all of the short-lived affairs and decadent parties. He could never be happy as long as there was a hole in his heart that, perhaps, he almost admitted to himself in the depths of his darkest moments, only she could fill. *'Maudlin rubbish'* he thought to himself sternly, *'no woman is worth it – I should thank her for showing me early what selfish whores all women are'*. He internally congratulated himself on the accuracy of this belief, noting that Blanchette had, after all, just proved its truth to him, yet again.

Taking another sip of his whisky, he steadfastly repressed the little niggle of doubt that scratched at the edge of his thinking, and leant back in the chair. But no matter what stern thoughts, the image of Honour's face would not leave his mind. He sat back in his chair, sighed, and let a single silver tear trickle down his face. *'Life'* he thought heavily *'life, life, life...'*

Chapter Two

"Oh Sissy!" exclaimed Beatrice, flicking her sandy hair idly like a girl of almost twenty years should only ever allow herself to do on special occasions.

"- will there be music, and dancing there tonight?" Honour could barely contain a heavy sigh and a frown at her younger sister's inane remarks. She had fielded questions of this nature all afternoon and was, by now, quite sick and tired of them. Her own adolescent enthusiasm for occasions such as that at the house of the Duke of Uxbridge, which they were planning to attend tonight, was now so distant that she could barely remember it.

Those lingering days of anticipation, the scent of powder and perfume as one gets ready, feeling the nerves in one's stomach as the maid pulled pinned and tucked into place the bodice of your best new frock.

Such notions Honour might have recalled had she been in the mood for sentiment. Beatrice however, had crushed such sentimentality, with her incessant wittering.

"…and will there be" Beatrice paused heavily at the word "-gentlemen present?"

"Yes, Beatrice, there will be. Unless that is, one of them hears you calling me 'sissy' and rushes off in horror at the thought of a silly little girl being in attendance at an occasion that is strictly reserved for grown-ups."

It almost hurt her to see Beatrice's sweet and serene face gradually turn more worried at her stern words, but she had endured enough today, and in the carriage on their way up from the country. It was time for a little sisterly revenge, so she went on –

"For there will also be punch there, and stronger drinks as well I'll wager, at least for the gentlemen. The eldest amongst them will want to discuss hunting, and cricket, and the Derby Stakes, and the best way to polish off a winged grouse - and the thought of giggling young girls will make them most displeased, and quite possibly a little vexed."

"Oh Honour, I cannot help it! I am just so happy to be in London at my first ball, I feel as if…" Beatrice paused a moment, looking for just the right words "… as if, were an especially powerful wind to come along, it would sweep me into the air by my petticoats!"

"Let us hope that no such occurrence comes to pass," Honour replied, maintaining her sternness, "- such a thing would be quite improper and I imagine people would talk."

'And aside from that', Honour thought to herself, uncharitably. *'It shall be my role tonight to ensure that no hyperactive young buck with a head full of the wrong sorts of ideas comes along and sweeps you off by your petticoats either...'*

Tonight Honour was to be a chaperone. For the first time in her life she had crossed the threshold. She had moved from willing young ewe, protected from the wolves on the perimeter of the flock, to the role of shepherdess, silently warding them off. Time had permanently changed her role, as it changes all things, and there was nothing to be done about it.

She looked at Beatrice with a strange mixture of yearning and envy. Never again would she be filled with such giddy feeling and innocent ideas, never again would she have to have an older relative beat aside handsome and willing suitors. It all saddened her too much, and she had no desire to go out to the ball tonight, or to endlessly hear of it from Beatrice.

Yet she had agreed to do just that.

Beatrice was Honour's sister. She had a brother as well, who, at thirty-one, was a year older than her and a commodore in the Royal Navy. She had grown up with him, Richard, grown used to his every frown and stench and passing fancy as only a sibling can, resenting and loving and ignoring him in equal measure. She had not, which the distance in their respective ages bore witness to, grown up with Beatrice. Beatrice had come later, eleven whole years later, by which time she and Richard were virtually adults (or so they thought!) and Beatrice was no more than a bawling swaddle of cloth for a nanny to take care of and for their mother to dote on.

There had been rumours around the estate, and whispered more quietly in the *ton,* of course. There always are, when a rich and well-bred woman births a child some years after her first brood have passed into adolescence. She was still just about fecund enough to plausibly manage it, but it seemed, to many onlookers, unlikely that the child had been sired by Sir Danvers Wormsley, their father. He had long since retreated into eccentricity and distance.

Beatrice was generally whispered of as the product of an affair, likely between her mother and a stable lad. It was a strange thought that had permanently distanced Beatrice from their family and community, although, being a naïve and self-contained girl, she had barely noticed the scorn her very existence had attracted.

Honour had never managed to deeply love Beatrice. She could pity her, sympathise with her strange existence - shut up in a cold country house with two ageing parents and a small staff - but love would have been far too heavy a label for any such feelings to bear the weight of. They had never been close, and had shared few of life's milestones in each other's company.

Before Beatrice was eight, Honour had been sent off to marry in any case. The Wormsleys had never been rich, but they had good pedigree and when a suitable man, the ageing Baron Fotherington, had taken a shine to Honour's red touched gold hair and easy vivacious nature, the match had been made and that had been that. She was given no choice, and the fact that she loved another was of no concern to her father.

The sisters parted company, seemingly forever, reunited briefly only on special family occasions and when an obscure relative had had the temerity to die.

Like her relationship with her sister, Honour's career attending balls had also been ended by her marriage to the Baron. He had doted on her, allowing her space, time to adjust to the life of a wife and then, hopefully, eventually mother, not minded her friendships with the servants, her greater interest in reading racy novels than in conversing with him, and even the short affair that she had carried on, discreetly, with one of the serving boys (a groom called Rogers, closer to her own age) in her second year as his wife. As long as she shared his bed, called him 'my darling' and kissed him on the cheek every night, the old man had been happy.

He was too fat and aged to sire any heirs, although he had, at first made some effort to do so, and despite (or perhaps because) of this, they grew to be relatively happy together.

She did, however, always wonder what would have happened if she had been able to marry James instead. But he had, it seemed, not felt her loss too badly, as he had gone off overseas within a short time after her marriage, and not come back for years. So perhaps, she told herself, she was better off without him.

Now though, Honour was a widow, of nearly two years, and widows need something to fill their days. She could not bring herself to sit at home all day, commanding her servants like an admiral on his quarterdeck, or re-reading the same limited selection of volumes, which Fotherington had provided for her.

So now, at her own mother's insistence, and to her little sister's eternal delight, she was sponsoring Beatrice's entrance into society, taking her out to find the charming, eligible young suitor that she herself had been denied.

There was a cruel irony to the entire enterprise, but then Honour supposed, that's life. No-one chooses their fate any more than they choose their station in society or the colour of their eyes.

"I cannot bring myself to take a final decision, Sissy!" Beatrice declared suddenly, after passing several minutes making vague pirouettes all over the drawing room floor, one dress or another held up against her.

"Should I wear the blue one, or the yellow one?" Beatrice glared at the frocks she had picked out for the evening, now lying on the bed where she had abandoned them, as if it were somehow their fault that she could not decide. Both were more than pretty and elegant, as far as Honour was concerned, and both had been paid for out of her late husband's generous endowment. Beatrice, 'little Sissy', as she liked to be called, knew nothing of such matters. As far as she was concerned, they might as well have materialised out of thin air, for her and her alone.

"I do not know, Bea" Honour said, allowing the affection she had somewhere deep inside her for her sister to come up, if only for a second. "I cannot possibly choose it for you. You must make your own decisions in these matters henceforth, if you are to be a lady of society. Discernment is most attractive in a woman." Beatrice gazed whimsically up at the white rococo ceiling. Up there, above the plaster, and the roof, and then eventually the clouds, there seemed to her to be a heavenly realm where every dream comes true and all gentlemen are decent, willing, and above all dashed good-looking.

To get to it, all she needed to do was pick the right dress, but the effort of the decision was so much that it caused her to screw up her face and dither for what felt like an age. *'If only'* Honour thought *'the most momentous decision of my life had simply been over a damned frock'*. She kept these words to herself, and allowed Beatrice to keep her illusions.

"I think I shall wear the blue one" Beatrice declared at last, with all the finality of a Roman Emperor. "It matches my eyes best."

"A very fine choice, my dear. The blue one it shall be".

Honour stood, and called for the maid to assist Beatrice with dressing for her first grand ball.

"Now I must go and prepare as well. Do try to sit still for Mary to dress your hair Sissy."

As Honour swept from the room, she wondered idly who she would see at the ball, what old acquaintance might be renewed, and what she might find to relieve the boredom of a life with no real direction.

Chapter Three

Blackwood almost forgot that he had been invited to a ball the next day. He woke sluggishly, having fallen asleep in his chair and slumbered fitfully for what felt like only a few hours. Stanford, his faithful London Butler, was standing over him, discreetly clearing away the mess of last night's drinking.

"I'm sorry to disturb you, sir" he said in his sombre, dedicated voice. "- I merely thought it best to remind you that you have an invitation to an occasion at Lord Uxbridge's residence in Belgravia this evening."

"I do?" Blackwood said, stuttering back to life. The taste of cigar smoke and whisky was thick at the back of his throat. He hacked up a cough to try and clear a path for his words. "- I must confess, I had entirely forgotten, thank you, Stanford."

"The pleasure of serving you is entirely mine, sir" Stanford replied, before ghosting away with a tray full of half empty glasses and cigarillo ends, mixed in with the carefully swept up fragments of a glass that James did not remember smashing.

James Blackwood did not make a habit of missing balls. When he had said that would be in attendance at a social occasion he attended, and did not like to pass up any opportunity for lively conversation or better, a seduction. The Duke of Uxbridge's ball would likely be one of the most fashionable of the season this year, and there was bound to be an ample selection of young ladies present, over whom he could exert his wiles and whom he could allow his reputation to entice.

Yet he could not help but feel a reluctance to go on this particular occasion, a withdrawn, wounded feeling that he had not felt since he was a youth. It was those thoughts of Honour, creeping back up on him, filling him with doubt, of himself, of society, of ladies and their innermost thoughts. He did not want to risk another humiliation like that which he had suffered up in Derbyshire - he needed to rest, recuperate and consider the situation.

There was also the horrifying fact that he would, he supposed, eventually actually have to marry one of the flittering young hopefuls, just so that he could father an heir. The thought was enough to make him truly wish to go nowhere near them.

It was no good however. Despite his fatigue and anxiety, Blackwood could not bring himself to face a quiet night in. After a short while sitting in the study, sipping coffee and trying to read to take his mind off affairs of the heart, women and his future, he resolved that he would face society once more.

How could he not? He was James Blackwood after all, the most notorious dandy in all the land, and he had a reputation to maintain. Quiet, last-minute cancellations did not emanate from his escritoire, when Blackwood was coming, he was coming, and he would dominate the hearts and minds of any social occasion for as long as he was in attendance.

All of these reminders, which had brought him great pride and comfort over the years, still gave him some sense of surety, but they were not the source of comfort they once had been. He needed a wife now, he thought, as he had last night, but there was only one possible way of getting one. It would be necessary to go out there and find a woman to fall in love with, or, at the absolute minimum, one that he could stand the thought of dealing with, for the rest of his life.

****

"... you have heard of me then?"

"Well yes!" the pretty young Lady Uxbridge tittered back "I shouldn't think there is a single person of any distinction in all of London society who has not heard of Mr. Blackwood!"

"I see. Then I suppose you have already formed some notion of my character and imprinted it firmly into your mind. I fear it would be futile,..." he said, eyeing her and letting his lips curl into a dark, cynical smile.

Her rich brown eyes dilated slightly as she contemplated him, fascinated, as young ladies so often were, by his aura, his presence, his history.

"… quite futile of me to offer even a token objection to that perception. I must confess that I am, as an old maid might choose to express it, 'bad to the bone' in your eyes, hmm?"

She laughed slightly, without breaking eye contact even for a single moment.

"Why of course not, sir!" she said, touching his arm gently, without really thinking about it. "I'm sure that the sort of salacious gossip one hears is wildly exaggerated!"

"Yes, I suppose you're right" he said, playing for humility. This was a routine so well-practised that he could do it without conscious thought or effort, the way a seasoned rider shifts their weight and the pressure of their lower body to command a horse. The thrill of it still brought him a little fluttering excitement, despite years of reputation.

"The question from your perspective surely has to be, in what direction the flow of exaggeration runs? Towards over-statement…" having turned away he now stared at her again, almost glaring, inviting her to stare at him and imagine him in all of his darkest and most dangerous moments. He was reeling her in, he could feel her heart heaving with the thrill of it beneath her fine evening gown "… or under?"

For a moment, the two were lost in each other's contemplation. The ball faded into the background, and all there was for either of them was the other's face, the point of access to their heart and soul and conscious mind. Blackwood reeled from it. This ball had been a dry disappointment up until now, had consisted largely of him skirting around the edges trying to avoid disapproving mothers, who chaperoned eligible young ladies, but now it was coming to life in his hand.

He still had his gifts, even still had his looks, and he was using them now with as much potency as ever before. The Duchess flushed, and fluttered her fan to cool herself as she considered the possible import of his words. He took advantage of the moment, smoothly, and with the ease of long practice.

"My Lady, are you well? It is such a crush, it is rather stuffy and overly warm in here – perhaps a turn on the terrace, to get some fresh air would help?"

She looked at him for a moment, considering, and even more flustered by his suggestion, and he simply took her hand, placed it on his arm, and escorted her towards the terrace doors. She was so overcome by his manner that she simply allowed him to lead her outside. Internally, he praised himself for his skill, and allowed himself to feel a little excitement about what he might be able to do with her next.

As a result, he was outside the room when the usher at the door announced the next arrival at the ball.

"Lady Honour Northbrook, Baroness Fotherington, and Miss Beatrice Wormsley, her sister" the announcement rang out across the room. Honour did not tarry at the entrance, but confidently led Beatrice towards a cluster of women at the other side of the room. Many of the male eyes in the room turned to regard her with as much. If not more, favourable attention as they gave her sister. Though a woman approaching middle age by the standards of the *ton* her looks and her figure were inordinately well-preserved. She had a clear, dark grey, eyes emphasised by her high cheekbones, and an almond-shaped, softly pale face perfectly set of by her pale green dress.

Her hair was a rich red-touched gold, and radiated warmth and vigour. She was oblivious to the attention that she was receiving, assuming, when she noticed anything at all, that the gentlemen's eyes were following Beatrice, who was quite beautiful, and radiant with excitement.

On the terrace, Blackwood's seduction of the Duchess was proceeding. He had led her to one side, to lean against the marble rail and look out across the gardens, where small lanterns were scattered artfully to enhance the view, without really casting much light at all. He moved closer to her, and slid an arm around her trim waist. She started at the contact, turning to him with eyes huge and round in surprise. The movement of her fan faltered, and she seemed frozen in place.

"Does the cool evening air help, my lady?" his enquiry was solicitous, and utterly ordinary in words, but his voice was low and seductive, and he pulled her ever so gently further against him. She resisted a moment then melted in his arms. He tilted his head down, watching her eyes all the while, and brought his lips to hers for a delicate, exploratory sensual kiss. She stilled, then, tentatively, responded. He exulted in the rush of energy that success always brought him, taking the kiss deeper for a moment, before drawing back to watch her face again.

She stood, her breath heaving, her eyes wide and her face flushed. After a moment, she seemed to come to herself, and suddenly pushed away from him, sliding from his grip.

"Oh… We shouldn't…. I didn't….. I don't….." her confusion was pretty and rather enjoyable. He went to draw her to him again, but she surprised him and twisted away, then simply turned and almost ran back to the doors, and disappeared back into the ballroom.

He paused, rather shocked. It was a long while since a woman that he wanted had got away from him that easily. Still, there was plenty of time yet – she had most definitely responded, had wanted the kiss, so a little further pursuit would surely bring the result that he wanted. An affair with the pretty young duchess would be a very pleasant dalliance.

Blackwood adjusted his cravat, settled his coat back to perfection, flicked his hair back into place, and went in search of a drink and possibly an hour or two in the card room with his friends.

He looked across the room, wondering how he could conceivable get to the drinks without being waylaid by someone that he did not want to talk to. Oh well, nothing for it, he launched himself into the sea of fluttering young things and predatory mothers. Working his way through the crush of people, he spotted Uxbridge, his host, talking to a woman in a pale green dress, right in his path to the refreshments table. Idly admiring her rather shapely rear view, he wondered who she was. He could hear snippets of their conversation as he approached.

"… well of course he shall be sorely missed. I passed many an enjoyable afternoon hunting with your good Baron Fotherington, and plenty of pleasurable evenings afterwards I do say. I am so sorry to hear of your loss."

"Your Grace is too kind," the woman replied. What on earth were they discussing? A death in someone's family? "- it has been a most sorrowful period, whilst it has been more than a year, I have simply not felt up to going out in society. Our physician had said the day might come soon, but no such foreknowledge can prepare one for such an event."

"I quite understand, my Lady, my sincerest condolences. Considering the circumstances, I am quite flattered that you are in attendance at all at our little occasion here. I should not have been in the least offended had you said you were unable to come."

"Not at all, Your Grace. Your balls are renowned throughout Europe for the generous hospitality of the House of Uxbridge! And I must think of young Beatrice, you understand…"

"Oh absolutely, a very commendable commitment to one's filial obligations! Now you must excuse me, I must attend to the Earl of Guildford who appears to be taking some rather considerable liberties with my punch bowl! My Lady…" and the Duke of Uxbridge flexed his enormous frame into a bow and made off in the direction of the punch, just as James reached the point immediately behind the woman that he had been speaking to. She stepped back, dipping an elegant curtsey to the Duke, and moving aside to allow him to pass.

That movement aside took her straight into Blackwood's path. Unable to stop, he collided with her, catching her elbow just in time to prevent the glass of ratafia that she held from being tipped rather disastrously over her beautiful gown.

She turned towards him, about to speak, whether to berate him or thank him he did not know, would never know. For when she turned and their eyes met, time stopped for both of them. It was, impossible as it seemed, Honour. Now only a few feet from the woman who had haunted his dreams for years he wondered how he could not have recognised her immediately, even when seen from behind, at a distance. She was, in so many ways, just the same, and more beautiful than ever.

She fairly shook with shock, but immediately regained her composure, at least a little, and pointedly detached his hand from her elbow.

Blackwood was transfixed, and the pretty Duchess Uxbridge whom he had just now been seducing, was quite forgotten.

They stood, staring at each other, both completely unsure, in that moment, how to go on, what to say. The thoughts raced through his head, an almost meaningless background noise, while his heart raced and his eyes remained captured by her – every detail seemed preternaturally clear – her slightly parted lips, the curl of her hair that twisted temptingly over her shoulder and drifted towards her breasts, spectacularly displayed by the elegant dress.

Blackwood realised that he was greatly pleased to see no sign of Baroness Fotherington's husband. The portly Baron had been an object of his private scorn for almost twelve years. That a chubby oaf like him could get to marry a woman of Honour's calibre, and without even having to demonstrate any virtue, or win her round at all had deeply offended him! The match had simply been arranged by Honour's assertive family, keen to secure for her a title and a match that would produce well-endowed heirs, and that had been that. Her scores of other, younger and more attractive suitors, a certain James Blackwood included, had been entirely left out of any consideration.

As with so many upper-class ladies, it was a question of either marry the best estate your family can find or do not marry at all. Honour appeared to be quite alone, which Blackwood found to be rather strange.

Had Baron Fotherington taken ill, or was he merely otherwise indisposed? Or could it be that the conversation overheard as he approached had concerned the death of Baron Fotherington?

He forced his mind to work, to focus on the now. He realised that he needed to speak, that if they stayed frozen in place like this, silent, the people around them would begin to notice, and quite likely a scandal would be created. He enjoyed being talked about – but only on his own terms, he had no interest in looking the fool before an entire ballroom.

"Baroness Fotherington, it is a great pleasure to see you once again" the greeting was perfectly sound, but Blackwood could not help but feel immediately that it was lacking something, that around this woman, he really ought to hold himself to higher standards of wit and charm, and say something more interesting. He contained the urge to wince, and kept up a polite smile.

"I can assure that you that feeling is *not* mutual, Mr. Blackwood. Rather a long time I fear, has elapsed since last we saw one another."

"Eleven years, I believe."

"Really? I was not aware that either of us might wish to so assiduously count the days and months since we last spoke. Though I am surprised that it is as long as that."

Blackwood felt foolish. A feeling that he did not welcome, and had not often experienced. He reminded himself that all women were faithless whores, this one most of all, and that he should not be surprised at her cold manner.

He wondered that the shock of finding her here had so rattled him that he had revealed so easily that, deep in his heart, he still felt something for her. He did not wish to, he had spent eleven years drinking her memory away, and he refused to be the target of her scorn again.

He resented his obsession with this woman, but he could not help it!

She had always stirred passions within him that he could not contain, and he was shocked to discover in this moment that she still did. Just her presence took his breath away, left him unable to find appropriate words, and he was intensely angry to discover that his usual calculated composure around ladies was crumbling in the face of her existence in the room.

"It was an approximate figure" he replied, a hard edge to his words, and then thought to add "- though a rather erratic one, I must confess. Is your honourable husband in attendance, my Lady?"

Once again his phrasing was crude, overly direct. He was spilling out his own thoughts when he ought to control them, and work them into subtleties.

It was just something that he could not, despite years of practice (eleven to be precise) seem to manage with Honour standing in front of him!

"No, I regret that he is not." A look of sorrow immediately came over Honour's face. She looked pale, ashen even, and for a moment regarded her shoes in a mild show of grief. "Baron Fotherington ended his tenure on God's good Earth a little over a year ago."

"Oh, my Lady! I am so sorry to hear it, please accept my condolences." Regardless of his ongoing belief that she was uncaring and greedy, like all women, the sight of what appeared to be true grief on her face had the power to move him.

This was an unexpected development, and it produced a mixed reaction in Blackwood. On the one hand, he knew now that Honour was available, so to speak, and might now be courted by all and sundry – a fact that he found disturbing, and unsettling, no matter how much he had sworn never to care for her again. On the other hand, he had just inserted another tactless remark into this already clumsy conversation, and internally winced at how poorly he was presenting himself.

"That will not be necessary, Mr. Blackwood" she said, terse and cold. She looked straight into him, with the piercing storm grey eyes that had so fascinated and shamed him as a younger man. Her dominance was already asserting itself, and he could feel it. Despite his years of hard-living seduction, he could not seem to exert any power over this woman and he was shocked to realise that, regardless of what he had told himself all these years, it just made him want her more and more.

"I appreciate your sentiments, but you must understand they bring me little comfort. Whilst I have passed the last eleven years happily, respectably married to a suitable and caring husband, you I understand, have made yourself notorious across the whole of Europe."

"One cannot always believe what one hears in whispered rumours at balls, or scrawled into the lower margins of the society pages."

He had mustered what he felt must surely be a good reply, some little flash of humour and warmth to break down Honour's hard exterior.

"No indeed, though I am a little perturbed that you presume those to be my principle sources of information on such questions. I have heard more than I should ever like to know about your misadventures abroad, your mistresses, your parties, if such occasions even deserve such a sobriquet, and your duelling, and I have been quite content for years that our correspondence ended when it did. It seems that circumstances intervened to save me from my own youthful foolishness. Now if you'll excuse me, it appears that my sister is in need of some rather more assertive chaperoning than present distractions permit me to implement. A good evening to you sir."

It was spoken in a tone that left him in no doubt that she had actually wished him anything but a good evening. She spun on her heel and walked off at once, so fast that it could almost be considered a public cut direct, leaving Blackwood entirely forlorn, confused, and alone.

Chapter Four

The next day Honour took tea at the house of her good friend Lady Fenway, in Fitzrovia. As the carriage bumped gently over the paved streets of London's west end, she was distracted from views of the handsome town houses and elegant parks, the great facades of the Royal Academy and the Hawksmoor churches, by thoughts of the previous evening.

It had not been a success, as far as her efforts to find a gentleman who might be a suitable husband for her sister were concerned. Beatrice was rather a shy girl, and though not plain not exactly pretty either. She had very little of her sister's gift for flirtation or invigorating conversation, and it had proven hard to get any of the distinguished young gentlemen present to take much of an interest in her. It had not helped that a number of the young ladies present at the ball had been quite stunning, and had drawn all eyes, making Beatrice look very plain by comparison.

A very handsome Naval Lieutenant, resplendent in his royal blue uniform, had spoken to her for a while, but had not, it seemed, asked her to dance, and she had been left for most of the evening on the margins, watching better-looking and more confident couples waltz and wheel in each other's arms whilst she nattered to a selection of new friends, all equally left on the sidelines. It was frustrating, but this was what Honour had agreed to. Sponsoring one's sister's entry into society had never been a straightforward or casual undertaking.

As the carriage drove past Bloomsbury Square Gardens however, Honour realised that this was not the principal aspect of Lord Uxbridge's Ball that was continuing to hold her attention. What she was really thinking about, frantically though she tried hard not to admit it to herself and had made active efforts to suppress such notions in her head, was James Blackwood, his reputation, his looks, their history. She could not quite fathom why it was that this disgraceful man, whom she had once thought herself desperately in love with, a long time ago, was now exercising such a hold over her imagination, yet he was. She had assured herself for years, each time she heard more of his scandalous life, that she had been well served by her father's insistence that she marry Baron Fotherington – saved in fact, from a potentially disastrous match, had she defied her family and run off with Blackwood (which she had, at least momentarily, considered).

Despite age diminishing his good looks and her knowledge that he was fundamentally a cad, especially in his dealings with the fair sex, she was intrigued by him, and wished, on one level, to see a little more of the man. She was disgusted with herself for it, but it was what she felt.

After her rather cold reception of him, he had stalked about alone for much of the evening, looking forbidding and dangerous, and then left early, without bidding anyone but his host farewell. She regretted, a little, her coldness, but at the same time it had been a frank articulation of how she felt. She was wary of him, and did disapprove passionately of what she had heard his habits of life had become.

Indeed, the reputation that Blackwood had garnered was in stark contrast to the shy and callow youth she had known all those years ago (all precisely eleven years ago, she remembered with amusement). She had been fond of him, in fact she had believed herself desperately in love with him, yet looking back at it, she realised that he had somehow lacked something, a gravitas, or an aura that might have made her fight to be with him. Or perhaps, she though with wry amusement, she had been just as shallow, and had lacked the courage to reach for what she wanted. No matter what his life had been since, she should not blame him for her own failings!

He had always been good-looking, indeed, when his face was fresher and his hair thicker, he had been among the most eligible bachelors in rural Derbyshire society, but she had felt at the time she had no choice but to comply with her father's wishes and reject his advances, though she had deeply resented being forced to that choice. To her, at the time, the fact that he did not try to convince her father to change his mind, and allow them to marry, had seemed to show a strange lack of conviction, a proof, to her younger self, that he had not really cared for her at all. She had been bitterly disappointed, and felt that his actions then, and the life that he had led since, surely supported her assumption.

As a girl, she had always imagined her future husband as not only handsome and well-bred, but also immensely sure of himself, a swelling tide that would sweep her up without thought or hesitation, a force of warm and passionate energy that could not be resisted. As a twenty-one year old, Blackwood had not been that, and so she had, when her father commanded it, terminated their correspondence, with some regret, feeling herself heartbroken, as much by what she saw as his betrayal of her, as by her father's refusal to consider her wishes.

Shortly afterwards she had complied with her father's wishes and married Baron Fotherington with good grace, if a depth of disappointment that her childish dreams would now never happen, and that had been that. She had lived very comfortably, and he had been a kind and doting husband, despite his advancing years and waistline. And now here she was, a widow, perhaps for the rest of her life, sponsoring and chaperoning the love affairs of other, younger women and watching on wistfully, comforted by a good circle of friends and her memories. It was not such a bad life, but not a terribly thrilling one either.

The carriage pulled into Great Portland Street and then took a sharp right onto Cleveland Street, at the entrance to Lady Fenway's house. It was one of the grandest, even in this especially affluent and well-regarded part of London, with its grand white façade, simply and tastefully plastered in the latest fashion. There were ornately gilded cast-iron railings curling about the entrance, conveying one up the small flight of stone steps that led to the grand doorway, itself painted a shimmering black.

The windows, square and perfectly uniform, seemed almost to glisten in a way that Honour was unused to, having spent most of her adult life in the provinces, where windows were a less acute indicator of one's means and status than they were here in the capital. The house, built at some point late in the previous century, was of five well-proportioned stories, square and lacking entirely in the sort of unsightly, unsanitary clutter so common in country houses. It was an ideal expression of the sensibilities of its time, clean, light and full of tranquil promise.

Honour was greeted with a well-practised bow by Lady Fenway's butler, Gateskill, and conveyed at once into the drawing room, where her hostess was waiting to receive her over a generous platter of tea and scones. She was struck immediately by the fashionable exoticism of the room, decorated with fine Japanese wall paper in jade and cream, with beautifully simple designs of bamboo trees and water lilies all around. The tea set too, was in a fine China porcelain of bright blue and white, radiating all the fine craft of the orient. Honour was immediately overcome by a desire to have such a room for herself, back in Sunderleigh Manor, the country home that her husband had been so gracious as to bequeath to her in his will. It seemed an ideal style for a room dedicated to relaxation and contemplation.

"My dear Lady Fotherington!" exclaimed Lady Fenway, rising to her feet to receive her guest. "So good of you to come around!"

"I'm delighted to be here my Lady!" she replied warmly. Lady Fenway was a firm friend of hers, and had been for many years. "… so good of you to have invited me, I see that you have re-styled the drawing room?"

"Yes, in the oriental fashion, Lord Fenway is determined that we keep abreast of all the latest styles. Many townhouses, I hear, have done the same, they're calling them 'Chinese drawing rooms' if you can believe it!"

"But of course, I had noted the rather eastern ambience immediately."

"Yes, I suppose that is the impression it's intended to convey. I was a little wary at first, at what exactly an oriental style of decoration would mean, being little versed in world affairs, but Charles insisted and I have to say, his judgement was not lacking, on this occasion at least."

"He has excelled himself, the room is utterly charming."

"You think so? It is very kind of you to say. We even acquired this China tea-set to go with it. I'm rather fond of the dragon you can see rampaging its way across the teapot, there."

"Yes, he is rather splendid isn't he?" as Honour contemplated the ornate eastern decoration of the tea-set, Gateskill, who, with the skill of all of the best domestic servants, had managed to blend so seamlessly into the background that she had hardly noticed him standing in attendance in the corner, came over and poured her a cup of tea.

"This is a new blend I was talked into by a tea merchant in Chelsea" said Lady Fenway as Honour took a sip. The tea was remarkable, unlike anything she had tasted before, with a distinct citrus note at the edges. "It's flavoured with something called Bergamot, a herb I believe. I'd never heard of it before but I must confess I've grown rather fond of this particular blend..."

"It's positively delicious" said Honour, eagerly taking another sip as Gateskill served her a scone, already laden with cream and rich, red jam. "- it is a terrible shame that living in the country, one is unable to keep abreast of London's cosmopolitan fashions. I feel really quite cut off from the world, living down in Sussex."

"My dear, there is no need to be!" replied Lady Fenway between mouthfuls of scone. Honour's host had never been one to starve herself, and was eagerly if still elegantly, demolishing the platter of scones now.

"You simply must invite me down, it feels like years since I last visited you at Sunderleigh! Society will keep up with you if you keep up with it, as my Aunt Ophelia always maintained. Considering it now past the year of mourning for your tragic loss, I think now is the time to start hosting once again."

"Yes, perhaps you are right" Honour said, suddenly a little forlorn at the thought of her widowed status. She realised with some shock that she really had no idea how to go on in society any more. It was true that she had not hosted even a modest party for many years now. As her husband had grown ill, she had largely cut herself off from her old circle of friends.

"On this particular occasion, I can say with some confidence that I am. And now seems as good a time as any to announce some news that I have concerning our little occasion here today."

"Oh yes?" Honour spoke quietly, recognising the tome in lady Fenway's voice, and already dreading what might come next.

Lady Fenway smiled rather coyly, and turned in her chair. Honour recognised these motions. Her friend had used to make them when she flirted with handsome gentlemen.

"Do you remember that rather quiet, dark-haired young fellow you used to associate with back in Derbyshire, a certain James Blackwood?" Honour froze for a moment in surprise, taking a shaky breath. What was this? What did Lady Fenway know about the two of them?

"Why, yes, I believe I do now remember him" she said, trying to keep her cool.

"Good, because I happened to cross paths with him only last week, when I was taking tea at Lord Redford's in Kensington. Still terribly handsome, and rather more self-assured now than he was, you might even call him charming. I understand he's acquired a somewhat rakish reputation, being a confirmed bachelor as he is, and spending a lot of time hosting out on his estate near Nottingham, but I should expect he's slowing down a little now, with age creeping up on him. Anyway, I got on with him rather well, and so I thought that I'd invite him over this afternoon, get the two of you re-acquainted as it were."

Honour was aghast. This was, to put it mildly, a most unexpected development. She had absolutely no idea how to respond, and the idea of seeing Blackwood again gave her cold shivers down her spine. Yet at the same time, she was just a little excited at the prospect, and thought that perhaps, should he behave suitably, she should make amends for her coldness the previous evening. The strange the things that can happen in London society, she thought! The links that are made without one's knowledge, the connections that you might never realise exist, between old friends and new.

There was, it seemed, no escape from her past. After years lived in the firm belief that he had never truly cared for her, and was quite the most reprehensible man alive, she was confronted with the disturbing possibility that it may not be as simple as that – that there may be a side to him that she had not known existed.

"Well there's no need to thank me! I'm sure you'll get on like the proverbial house on fire! He should be here any minute now…" and, as if to re-emphasise the role of fate in all of this, at that precise moment there was a knock at the door. With singular swiftness, Gateskill was in attendance, the door was answered, there was the sound of boots pacing confidently across the parquet floor, and within a handful of heartbeats Mr James Blackwood was once again standing in front of Lady Honour Fotherington, wearing a rich chestnut brown dress coat and with his hair sitting thick and curled atop his head. Almost, for a moment, he looked just like his younger self, but with an added air, a strength or certainty, a greater confidence in himself, perhaps.

"My Ladies" he said in the husky voice that had conquered a thousand hearts in all the great houses of Europe and beyond. "- so very kind of you to receive me in such auspicious surrounds" he gestured to the oriental wallpaper, clearly as struck by it as Honour had been. Her heart and mind were racing so fast in tandem that she could barely bring herself to look at him. She feared either breaking out in girlish flushes of embarrassment, or else staring into his soul with a look of fierce wariness that he would interpret as disapproval. She had, she realised in that instant, no idea whatsoever how she felt about him, what she now believed of him.

As she often had in the past, she let Lady Fenway do the talking.

"Yes, Baroness Fotherington was just remarking on the new oriental approach we've taken to the withdrawing room. Do you think it a little ostentatious, Mr. Blackwood?"

"Why, on the contrary Lady Fenway" he said, making her feel that he was taking her into his confidence, as he seemed able to do with everyone save Honour. "It is quite a match for the charming company I am so blessed to find myself in."

"Oh Mr Blackwood!" Lady Fenway giggled. If Honour didn't know any better, she would have suspected the two of them of flirting. She had not yet met Blackwood's gaze, and decided it would be prudent not to until he addressed her directly. The circumstances were too complex for an ordinary reaction of modesty and politeness. "- you are as ever, simply too kind in your praise, may I offer you a cup of tea?"

"I would be honoured", he sat down next to Honour, and waited for Gateskill to serve him. Inwardly Honour berated herself for having had the stupidity to sit on a couch which provided the opportunity for someone to sit beside her.

She knew that he was sitting at a perfectly suitable distance from her, well within the bounds of propriety, yet somehow she could feel his presence – an alarming sensation of almost physical heat that seemed to wash over her body from his direction.

She could feel him looking at her, burning a momentary gaze into her right cheek, but she did not turn to look at him.

"I believe you are already acquainted with Baroness Fotherington here, although you may previously have known her as Miss Honour Wormsley, before her marriage."

"Certainly, Baroness Fotherington and I have an established acquaintance of, oh I don't know, around eleven years." He smiled at her, and she blushed a little half-smile back, surprised to find that, without having intended to at all, she had somehow raised her eyes and turned to look at him.

"... indeed we were only discussing that fact last night, at the Duke of Uxbridge's Ball in Mayfair."

"You were both in attendance at His Grace's ball? Why did you not say so, my Lady!"

"I had not yet had the opportunity to say as much" said Honour, slightly perturbed at being forced to admit to her social habits. "- but yes, Mr. Blackwood and I had the opportunity to renew our acquaintance, as he says, after eleven years, only last night."

Her eyes met Blackwood's, and despite herself, and the surroundings, she felt herself drawn towards him.

For just a moment, a feeling she had not felt since she was a girl fluttered and quivered inside her. He held her gaze with an ease that he had not possessed last night, and had never had as a young man, but which she now found compelling. What a strange turn of events!

"Well, I should imagine that you had plenty to talk about, reminiscing about your youth back in Derbyshire?" said Lady Fenway, sensing the undercurrent of tension in the room, and perhaps regretting her decision to engineer this reunion.

She was, however, one of those experienced hostesses who are gifted at keeping conversations light and convivial, and was doing her best to do so now.

"Indeed, we did have plenty to discuss, though Baroness Fotherington was a little too preoccupied with her sister to indulge in sentimentality and nostalgia", said Blackwood, a slight edge to his voice, not taking his deep, dark eyes off Honour for a second.

She could feel herself outmanoeuvred. This was a very odd social situation, one she had not been at all prepared for.

"Yes, I was there to attend to Beatrice's entrance into society, and that absorbed the great bulk of my attention." She turned to face him with a steely look, a look that said "work for my approval, or even my acceptance." Blackwood simply turned away.

At that moment, Gateskill stepped back into the room, once again moving almost as silently as it was possible to move.

"Begging your pardon my Lady, but there is a tradesman here at the rear entrance here to discuss the rhododendron bed?"

"Oh, dear, I'd entirely forgotten! How terribly embarrassing, I shall have to attend to this for a few moments. Do excuse me..." and suddenly Lady Fenway bustled off, leaving the two of them alone in one another's company.

For what was probably only a few seconds, but felt like several agonising lifetimes the two simply sat, and looked at each other, bemused, bewildered, and it seemed, equally completely unsure what to do.

Then, at last, Blackwood spoke.

"How strange that we should have been parted for so long, and then find that we chance upon one another twice in the same number of days."

"Yes, I must confess, it is a little odd," Honour replied. "I am rather unsure of what to make of it."

"There is much in our past that could be considered.... unresolved.... that appears to be compelling the two of us together." Blackwood spoke boldly, sitting bolt upright on the couch as if nervous tension ran electric through his body.

He had moved closer to Honour, and though she did not recoil, she felt a little strange, a little flushed, and perhaps almost a little shaky.

"And, sir, let us not forget, plenty that has kept us apart, further and further apart as time went on. That still keeps us apart I believe, in our manners and habits of life, in the way that we structure our days and the company that we keep in private."

He felt her words like a slap to his face.

For she was right.

He could no longer lie to himself – his habits and friends of the last ten years or more were, when seen through the clear filter of her perception, completely reprehensible.

In that moment he hated himself, even more then he had been doing so of late.

It was one thing to consider these things in his most private thoughts, in the small sleepless hours of the morning – quite another to face them head on, when they were thrown in his face by this woman.

He felt his carefully constructed wall of beliefs, which had protected him from the world for so long, crumbling in the face of her words. And through that crack in his armour, came another unwanted thought – what if he had been wrong about her?

What if she was not the unfeeling bitch that he had seen in his mind, since that day when she turned from him to marry an old man with money? What if she was not the greedy whore he had deemed her? He shuddered slightly, becoming aware that he had been silent too long.

Honour was looking at him, one golden eyebrow slightly raised, seemingly rather puzzled by his silence. He found himself captured by those stormy grey eyes, his breath coming short and his heart beating faster.

A sudden, completely unexpected impulse took him, and, before he could stop to think, he grasped her hand between his and spoke.

"Oh Honour! My years of notoriety have been nothing, nothing but a hollow effort to fill the hole that you left in my heart!"

His words shocked him – they were nothing like those he had considered speaking, when he chose to accept Lady Fenway's invitation. It appeared that they shocked Honour just as much, for she sat up straighter and stared at him in amazement.

Honour was, indeed, utterly shocked by this turn of events.

This was a bizarre and unexpected turn, and she wished only for Lady Fenway, or at the very least Gateskill, to come in now and interrupt this unwanted outpouring.

Nonetheless, she found her heart beating harder, a warmth spreading through her from where his hands held hers. Could what he said be true?

Was it possible that he was not the hard-hearted, uncaring rake that she had believed he was, since that day eleven years ago, when he had left the country without even sending her a message?

"Honour, I see now that you are the only woman I have ever actually loved, I ……." He got no further with his impassioned speech, and was, in a sense, grateful to have his words cut off, as the turmoil in his thoughts intensified.

"Sir!" she exclaimed, pulling her hand away. "As flattered as I am by the strength of your passions I think them most improper! You dishonour our temporarily-absent hostess, and the memory of my husband, with this display!"

"But …." Words failed him and action took over - he moved closer, and bent to her, seeking to lay a kiss on her cheek, but she turned away swiftly, rising to her feet, resisting his impetuous advance.

He was shocked all over again.

He was not used to rejection by women, in fact, he realised, darkly amused by the thought, this was the only woman who had ever thoroughly rejected him, and here she was, doing so again!

"Mr. Blackwood, you must understand, I cannot consider this!" she said tersely, imploring him, moving unthinkingly towards the wall to get away from his proffered embrace, his lips and hands.

"- I regret the nature of our parting all of those years ago, and, now that you have forced such a confession from me with this display, I concede that you have enjoyed a small but lingering place of affection in my heart. But do not presume that, simply because I have recently lost a husband, I am now on the prowl for a ready replacement! I am here to sponsor my sister, not to be denigrated as one of your..." the word was there, but at first she dared not speak it.

She knew however, that she must sink to a level of bluntness that this man's man, this cad (for she could not believe that what he said was true – surely not!) whom she saw before her, staring imploringly at her with his sad, dark eyes, would understand. "...one of your whores!"

She immediately regretted the word. Never in all of her life had a single syllable from her mouth caused such immediate distress.

Blackwood seemed at once to deflate, slumping back into his chair, his eyes glazing over with a sorrowful film, his lust immediately checked, denied, and set aside. She had never seen such a rapid change in a man.

"You are right of course", he said, in a heavy, resigned tone. "It was disgraceful of me to behave as I just did. I am forced to confront a clear reality - I am a dishonourable bounder, infamous across the civilized world, while you are a fine and respectable woman of society. I was in error, and I apologise."

He rose to his feet, buttoned his coat and breathed deeply, as if about to face some great challenge he was steeling himself for. Honour, in her turn, sat back down, and despite everything, from Blackwood's reputation to the absurd nature of his outburst, she felt a sadness for him, not pity as one feels for a wounded child, but rather an empathy, a realisation that, unsettling as the thought was, perhaps they shared a similar weight in their souls. They each, it seemed, had harboured strong feeling for each other over all of these years, even if she had believed that her feelings for him were closer to hatred than love. Perhaps, she was startled to realise, that had not been the truth, but merely her way of dealing with heartbreak. She pushed that thought away, firmly. No matter that his dark good looks and roguish charm held a certain appeal, she would not expose her heart to such risk again.

"Thank Lady Fenway for the tea, and for her splendid company. I am afraid..." he fumbled for an excuse "- that I have urgent business to attend to, and shall have to depart at once for The City. Please convey my regret at the sudden adjournment of our little gathering. I don't suppose you and I shall see one another again. Farewell." And, without any further ado, he pivoted on the spot, and showed himself out, into the streets of Fitzrovia, leaving Honour to ponder what might have been, years ago, and feeling a nagging regret that this might indeed, be the last time they met.

Blackwood had hoped that Mademoiselle Jauzion's company would take his mind off Honour, but like drinking, gambling, and carousing with his usual companions, it had proven inadequate. He was back in Nottinghamshire, on his country estate, for yet another weekend of debauchery, arranged at the last minute to try and help him to get over his awkward afternoon in Fitzrovia.

Tomlinson, Travers and Cranston had all come up, accompanied by their mistresses, and a selection of disreputable types from the London theatres, who Blackwood had intermittent contact with. Among these was Mademoiselle Jauzion, the toast of all the darkest London bordellos, a singer, actress and courtesan of considerable renown with whom he had shared many nights of passion. This time however, it simply hadn't been enough.

He rolled over, on his well-used four poster bed, and decided to try once again. She was there, lying before him, entirely naked and completely available, a woman capable of provoking lust in even the sternest bishop, but, though he felt a base, animal desire nagging at him, once more Blackwood felt only shame at what he had done, and continued to do. He shoved the feeling aside, and reached for her, locking all thought of Honour, and love, into the deepest recesses of his mind. He was James Blackwood – he had a reputation to maintain!

"Encore, ma chérie?" she cooed, as his hands worked their way across her breasts and a low tingling ran between the two of them, desire rising in its wake. His palm flattened against the small of her back and dragged her closer, drawing a slight practiced giggle from her as a sharp burst of anticipation stiffened her spine, arching her body against his. He could see all the goose-pimples on her perfectly clear skin, the burning hardness of her little, shockingly rouged, nipples, the fine silky hairs on her arms all erect before him, saluting him and him alone, but annoyingly, again, his thoughts turned to Honour. He had never seen her like this, never heard this tone of voice come over her from the other side of the pillow, never been overwhelmed by her low groans and fluid motions. It pained him, but all he could think to do for now was to kiss and grope at Mademoiselle Jauzion, seeking to bury his feelings as he buried his cock inside her.

"Ah, oui, oui, embrasses moi, comme ca, comme ca" his lips tightly against her neck, he sucked away hard until he was almost biting her, as he held her firmly and thrust himself hard into her lithe body.

She exhaled sumptuously into his ear, and their tongues clashed almost in mid-air as he paused a moment, fully sheathed within her, before the two of them being well-versed in the each other's expressions of passion, their bodies began to move as a singularity, caressing, thrusting themselves into a new indulgence in intimacy. As was her custom, Mademoiselle Jauzion began to exclaim in her own language

"Baisses moi! Baisses moi! Comme ca, comme ca, oui monsieur comme ca!" this habit usually brought Blackwood to a fever pitch of desire, overwhelming his senses, but on this occasion he felt numb. He continued, thrusting against her until the final, halting cessation, but he felt little from it.

He turned over and stared at the ceiling darkly, trying to compose himself once more. After a few moments of heavy breathing recovery, his French mistress put her arms over his chest and started to probe.

"You are a little different this evening, Monsieur Blackwood?" she said, her Parisian accent drawing out the final syllable of his name in a manner he had always found strangely comic. He had never been able to decide whether the French habit of talking at great length before, during and after love-making was preferable to the English rectitude or not. It certainly made the whole experience smoother, but robbed it of a certain mystery.

"Is something, er, how you say, 'on your mind'?"

"I don't know Sylvie", he said, even huskier than usual, as he usually was after making love. "I'm sorry, it's a little complicated." She smiled, and turned onto her front.

She had always liked to do this, probing the minds of her lovers in a haze of post-coital satisfaction. Blackwood wasn't sure how much he felt comfortable confessing.

"You can tell me, it is quite alright", she said, pleasantly.

She might be a whore, but she was certainly a friendly whore, when it came down to it. She had enough self-confidence, and enough admirers queued up seeking her favours, that she felt no insecurities – whatever her lovers may confess, she was quite certain that any problem would be with them, not with her performance.

"What is troubling my big, strong English man?" she fondled his chest and arms, and drew the confession out of him.

He had never met anyone with such an immediate understanding of the patterns of the male mind.

"It's all quite straightforward really. But it's also entirely hopeless. There's no escaping it I'm afraid, Sylvie, I am suffering for love, and for my foolish behaviour long ago."

"Ah!" she fairly cried at once, "- well that is not so bad a thing after all! In fact, love, it is a rather wonderful thing, though often a little hard, or how you say - *compliqué* at the start. And, surely, any behaviour from long ago, no matter how bad, can be forgotten, left behind in time, *n'est ce pas*? Who is the woman?" she eyed him playfully, her full, ruby red lips curving into a smile "- it is not me, is it? Because I am afraid I would have to say, there are already too many men in love with Sylvie Jauzion! I would have to put you at the back of the, er, the queue as it were, hmm?"

He laughed at her flirtatious allusions. She was as vain as any actress could be expected to be, but her self-awareness made her all the more attractive.

"No Sylvie, I'm afraid it is not you."

"Ah, *quelle dommage*! How I love to be loved! Then if not me, she must be a very beautiful woman, *ma chérie*, very beautiful indeed. Who is she?"

Blackwood instinctively sighed, and the smile that Sylvie had drawn across his face dropped. It was difficult owning up to this, even in private and to a woman in whom he had confided many times in the past, albeit never anything like this.

"Her name is Honour Northbrook, Baroness Fotherington. I have known her since I was a boy. We courted once, briefly, but she married a Baron over twice her age, many years ago, and we lost touch. She is widowed now, but I fear..." he could almost feel a tear pricking up in the corner of his eye, how maudlin of him!

This was unprecedented, James Blackwood did not cry! He had not cried since he was but a callow and unbroken youth, not even on the day when he was told that Honour would not see him, and that she was to marry another!

It took a titanic effort of will to contain his sudden desire to burst into tears. "... I fear the feelings for her that I have preserved, no matter how hard I tried to expunge them from my heart and mind, for nearly twelve years are not entirely reciprocated."

He sniffed slightly, choking back the urge to cry.

"Now that I have met her again, I can see that, perhaps, all of things that I have believed about her, since she turned from me to marry another, may not be entirely true. But she can only see that I left her with no message, upon hearing of her betrothal, and simply immersed myself in travel, and in being as uncaring and wild a rakehell as I could find a way to be. She rightly despises me for the way that I have behaved, and wishes not to ever see me!"

Sylvie, well-used to gentlemen who became tearful after a session in bed, put her arms around him and offered a deep, warm smile.

"Oh, monsieur, it is a painful situation, the unrequited love. But it is something that we all must face, *non*? It is part of life, we fall in love, sometimes the other person feels same way, sometimes no, it happens, even to a beautiful and acclaimed *actrice* like myself."

"I find that extremely hard to imagine."

"Oh, but monsieur, I do not lie! Why before I came to London, I was deeply in love with this man, Jean-Luc Plisson. He was the most celebrated actor in all of Paris in the time of Napoleon, he had women chasing him through the streets and lining up around the corners of the theatres just to catch a glimpse of his wonderful face, his incredible charm. I was in a play with him, and we kissed one night backstage, and I thought that was it, that was love, but he did not love me back, he carried on his affairs with his mistresses, he did not even look at me again. I was so heart-broke, could not sleep, I could not eat. In the end, to get away, you understand, I come to England! Now everybody loves me!"

"It would seem that our lives' histories are not so very different, Sylvie."

"But of course! I have always felt this about you, monsieur Blackwood, that there is something of the adventurer to you, but that, like all adventurers, your wandering, your womanizing, it come from a deep pain within you, *non*?"

"I suppose you are right. This is a painful truth for me to confront, but confront it I must. You seem to have seen right through me, right into my very heart and soul. But what am I to do?" She gave a slow, Gallic shrug, and regarded him frankly.

"Of course there is not always anything to be done, when you love someone and they do not love in return. You can make your feelings clear, and behave with dignity and honour. That is all that there is to be done."

"You are right. Thank you, Sylvie. I think I shall be returning to London a little sooner than I had planned."

Blackwood turned away from his French confidant, and without any more need for human contact, slept deeply for many hours. It was the first dreamless sleep that he had experienced for some years, and that realisation shocked him, when he awoke, alone, the next morning.

Chapter Six

Honour sighed, letting her fork fall back onto her breakfast plate and ignoring the barely touched food that she had been pushing around for half an hour. Beatrice, completely oblivious to anything but her own thoughts, was wittering on incessantly about all of her totally unsuitable suitors. The detailed comparison was utterly boring, from Honour's point of view, as they were all UNSUITABLE!

It did not help that there was yet another ball tonight, as there had been every night, and that Honour's level of interest in attending was zero. Also, if she was to be honest with herself, she was decidedly out of sorts and irritable as a result, no matter how much she tried to repress that inappropriate and unladylike behaviour. She was short on sleep, not just because of the exhausting social schedule, but, she was chagrined to admit, even to herself, because her thoughts were haunted by one touch.

Once the shock had worn off, she had not been able to stop thinking about that moment in the drawing room at Lady Fenway's, when James Blackwood had taken her hand in his, and declared his longstanding affection for her. Most especially, she recalled the curious warmth that had crept through her, emanating from his hands where they held hers.

Her breath had caught, and her heart beat faster at the time. She had been at once horrified and fascinated by his behaviour. There was such an echo of the passionate boy that he had been when they had thought themselves in love, all those years ago. Suddenly she could see that boy before her, strengthened and sharpened by the years in between – callow promise become a handsome, powerful man. A powerful man, who, in that moment, appeared to have been almost broken by her words.

That had shocked her too – that, it seemed, she had such power over him. She was not sure if she wanted that power, intoxicating as it had been for a moment. Each night when she had lain down to sleep, she closed her eyes, only to see in her mind, that moment, to feel that touch, that heat that seemed to flow between them, through the layers of their gloves, as if they touched, skin to skin. She tossed and turned, unable to sleep, feeling the stirring of passions in her body that had been long repressed, put aside after the disappointment of her clandestine couplings with nervous, inexperienced Rogers, and after poor dear Fotherington became.... incapable... as his illness progressed.

In so many ways, her experience of the passions of the body was limited, and she found the idea of James Blackwood, a renowned rake and seducer, both tempting and frightening.

The fact that one moment of touch had left her in such turmoil scared her, yet she could not push the thoughts aside. He had seemed, in that moment, so genuine. Could it be that she had wronged him in her thoughts, these eleven years past? What if he had truly loved her, but had simply not had enough power and influence to be able to challenge her father? What if she had seemed to him to not care, to have cast him off in favour of Fotherington's money? All these years she had thought him uncaring – had he thought the same of her?

Should she have fought harder, argued with her father's choice? Honour did not know, but was left with an increasing feeling of guilt, and horror at what she and James seemed to have wrought between them – for him, years of philandering, debauchery, drink and gambling, all trying to forget her, and for her, years of bland nothingness in a kind but loveless marriage, feeling the brightness of her life bleed away into grey by the day, all to forget him. Yes, she finally admitted it. She had been trying to forget, to convince herself that she was correct, that he did not care, so that she could justify her choice of a life of stultifying boredom.

What sleep she had was broken, and her mood and patience became steadily worse as the days passed. She did not know what to do. Which was not at all a sensation that she was used to.

To make matters worse, Beatrice appeared to have a spectacular talent for attracting the wrong sort of suitor, and her work as a chaperone was not so much fending of terrible rakes (although there were a few) but rescuing Beatrice, at regular intervals, from crashing bores. And this morning, her head ached.

Beatrice finally noticed Honour's silence and stillness, and her chatter wound down. She fixed Honour with a curious look and, tentatively, asked;

"Sissy, are you well? You're very quiet, and you look, now I think about it, very pale."

Mentally gritting her teeth, Honour forced herself to smile, and replied, as lightly as she could, "I am afraid that I have rather a megrim this morning. It is making me feel very out of sorts. I believe that I will retire to bed for a few hours, with one of cook's excellent possets, and make sure that it improves before this evening's ball."

"Oh yes! Please do that, you just simply must be well for this evening! I shall spend the day reading and embroidering, don't worry yourself about me." Beatrice's face shone with genuine care, only slightly underlaid with a selfish wish to have nothing stop her from attending the evening's ball.

After sending a footman to the kitchens to request that cook send up the posset with one of the maids, Honour retreated to the quiet of her room. Surely she would be able to sleep now, she was so very tired.

She sat on the bed, leaning back against a pile of pillows and closed her eyes against the throbbing pain. Immediately, as if imprinted on the inside of her eyelids, the image of James' face, dark eyes full of hurt at her words, rose before her. She wished, oh how she wished, that she could go back to that moment and say something different.

It did not matter what his behaviour over the years, she was, after all, now almost certain that all of that could be laid at her door.

She was almost certain that her actions had caused him to be so, as much as his own actions, but it only mattered that she wipe away that genuine hurt from his eyes, now. It seemed likely that she would never get another good night's sleep again, unless she could do that, could atone for her harsh words in some way.

A tap on the door, and Jane brought her the warm posset, placing it carefully on the little table beside the bed. Honour sent her away with thanks, asking her only to return in time to help her dress for this evening's ball. The posset helped with the megrim, but not with sleep, or her persistent thoughts of James Blackwood.

Eventually, she could stand it no more, and, in her desperation to find a way to change what had happened, she came to a decision. A decision rather lacking in propriety, and somewhat outrageous for her, who was usually so very well behaved, but one which she felt might actually achieve the result that she desired. *And what result is that?* Her inner voice asked. She pushed the question aside, not willing to look at it too closely, and moved to act on her idea before she lost the courage to do so.

Honour sat at the little writing desk under her window, and stared at the sheet of paper before her. Closing her eyes a moment, she took a deep breath, then opened them, fixed the paper with a steely glare, as if it might attempt to escape her words, and began to write. Fifteen minutes later, after many pauses for thought, and much chewing at her lower lip in concentration, she was done. She signed it with a flourish, sanded it dry, folded and sealed it, then carefully inscribed its direction on the outer surface.

Taking a deep breath, she put it to one side, carefully hidden beneath her book, and stood to stretch, just as Jane arrived to help her dress for the evening. She had not slept, but, she realised with surprise, she felt much better, able to face the evening's social whirl, somehow more at peace within herself.

Smiling, she turned to choose a gown for the evening, eventually settling on a rich green dress, elegant in its simplicity. She had chosen to leave, for tomorrow, the fashionable new gown in a pretty light gold, with shimmering lace over satin, and delicate embroidery on the small sleeves and bodice, set off by a sash beneath her bust, in a reddish gold tone that perfectly set of the red highlights in her gold hair. She knew exactly why she wanted to wear that tomorrow. She smiled again, and gave herself over to Jane's ministrations, actually rather looking forward to this evening, and, perhaps, more so to tomorrow evening.

An hour later, on her way out the door, she passed a sealed missive to the footman, requesting that he have it delivered with all haste.

Blackwood did not regret his decision to leave Nottinghamshire for the capital. He entrusted his house to his ever loyal (and mercifully discreet) domestic servants, and to Travers, whom he knew he could trust after all these years, and went back to try and conceive of some way of winning his way back into Honour's affections, or, at minimum, finding a way to at least obtain her friendship, rather than her disdain, no matter how much he might deserve the latter.

It would be no easy task, and there was no guarantee of success, but, as the carriage rumbled through the fertile flatlands of the east Midlands, the bleak expanses of the Fens, and then finally the gently rolling hills and plump, prosperous little villages of the Home Counties outside London, he knew that the determination he felt swelling in his heart was a sign.

He had been looking for a way out of this life that he had built for himself, he had finally admitted. A way to no longer be trapped by that reputation that he had built so assiduously, never foreseeing the day when he would find it so constricting, and so far from how he wished to live.

Becoming a despised, ill regarded aging roué, had no appeal whatsoever, now that he was old enough to see that somewhat closer on the horizon.

Whilst it was painful in the extreme to admit that, all these years, he had been deluding himself, and blaming everything on Honour, in fact, on all women, Honour's words at Lady Fenway's had, in an instant, flipped his perception around – he could see, in excruciating clarity, that from Honour's position, it appeared that everything was a result of his uncaring behaviour, his lack of courage, and love. To her, it seemed that he had abandoned her without a word, not caring enough to fight for her, and had run, to a life of unredeemed, and unrepentant, bad behaviour of all kinds.

Honour was, truly, the only woman that he had ever loved, although in his callow youth he had not been perceptive enough to see what a marvellous gift was presented to him – in this world of loveless marriages, he had been given the chance to marry for love, if only he had tried – and he had thrown it away. She was, he now admitted, the only woman for him. His current state of bachelorhood was directly related to that, not just because he had chosen to despise all women in his sulky, bitter reaction, but because, in truth, he had never met another woman that he could actually even vaguely contemplate living with, as man and wife.

He was resolved: he would pursue her until he either had what he wanted, or could do no more and was able to force himself to accept that he must live on as a bachelor, getting old disgracefully in private. That thought now rather terrified him, but he had to face the fact that, in Honour's eyes, he was likely beyond redemption, and that he may never receive a civil word from her again.

His townhouse in Holborn proved a welcome refuge when he arrived, greeted by Stanford with a solemn bow and a plate containing a letter, addressed directly to him. Intrigued, he tore it open and read

Dear Mr. Blackwood,

I felt that I must take the unconventional step of presuming on our acquaintance and writing to you directly. I pray you forgive my break from propriety in this matter. You see, I regret my rather terse and defensive manner with you the other afternoon. You must understand that I am in a rather delicate state of mind at the moment, considering my need to adjust to widowhood, and to deal with the demands of launching my sister into society, hence my mind has been distracted.

Please excuse my harsh words as a consequence of my shock at both your presence at lady Fenway's, and at your very much unexpected words. I wish to reassure you that you do occupy a place of affection in my heart, and that I have cherished fond memories of our youthful acquaintance over the past years (eleven years, to be precise).

Though I cannot bring myself to condone your behaviour at Lady Fenway's last week, I also regret my rather impulsive reaction. It was wrong of me to turn you away so suddenly and unfeelingly, and I apologise. I see no reason why we cannot, at the very least, be warm friends heading into the future.

It is to this end that I am side-stepping conventional social formality somewhat in inviting you to accompany myself and my sister, Miss Beatrice Wormsley to the Earl of Kidderminster's forthcoming ball, the evening of the 28th of June.

I shall have my footman collect you on our way, if that suits, and make the necessary arrangement to inform our host of your attendance. Please let me know if such an arrangement would be inconvenient to you, though I must say that I hope that you can attend. I should like to go some ways to repairing my cold treatment of you on our previous two encounters.

Yours,

Lady Honour Northbrook,

Baroness Fotherington

Despite himself, Blackwood was simply incandescent with joy. He felt like grabbing old Stanford, who had offered him the letter so soberly, and kissing him passionately by way of a thank you. This was perhaps the happiest a letter had ever managed to make him, for Honour was thinking about him, and sending letters to convey her affections! He had hoped for far less on the drive down to London, this was a most auspicious greeting! Still, he sternly repressed his immediately joyous reaction — after all, she simply spoke of being friends, and he still hoped for so much more.

The scope of a lifetime of loneliness still stood, like a spectre, awaiting him.

The letter had arrived just in time, for the ball was taking place tonight. His decision to leave Nottingham rather suddenly was vindicated, and Blackwood could not help but see some small degree of fate in the resolution he had made after his conversation with Sylvie only three nights ago.

Perhaps on some profound, spiritual level he had known all along that these were the contents of Honour's mind, and that it would only be right and proper for him to be on hand in London to receive them. In his thoughts, he rather laughed at himself, seeing a giddy boy in his reactions – so far from the sartorially sarcastic and cynical person that the *ton* saw him as.

In any case, he thanked the God that he had not worshipped, or even thought about for years, and whom he privately believed might not even be there, for having guided him back to this note.

The wording of it was equally intriguing to him. In particular the passage where she said "I see no reason why we cannot, at the very least, be warm friends". At the very least! What on earth did that mean? Was that an allusion to her true feelings, to a burgeoning attraction it would only take repeated contact, and a little charm, to develop into a full-blown passion?

Despite his thirty-two years, James Blackwood was consumed by the letter like a feverish adolescent hearing from their sweetheart for the first time. He could not quite believe it, and neither would any of his friends.

He was, he realised, completely, dramatically, utterly in love with Honour.

He felt rather foolish admitting it to himself, and the feeling was so inextricably tangled up with his feelings of shame and anger that had driven his years of debauchery that he did not know how to deal with the tumble of emotion in his mind.

He was also deeply aware that, if he even mentioned his thoughts to his closest friends, they would scoff, and back away in horror, certain that he had, this time, lost his mind.

A further piece of amusement at his own expense resulted, when he realised that he now felt a certain sympathy for old Henley, pompous letter notwithstanding, living in the country, and besotted with his young wife.

He drifted about the house, entirely distracted, for nearly an hour. The time streaked past him like a bird on the wing, he was wandering through the library one moment and staring out the window in his study the next, mind full of thoughts of Honour, and not much else, not thinking for a single moment about how he must appear or what any idle observer might think if they were to catch sight of him.

He lost track of the passing of time to such an extent that he had to hurry his valet, Buckham, along to dress him. Buckham gave him the strangest look when that hurry-up was accompanied by an apology for the lateness of the request.

It was not the sort of thing that James usually did – apologising to his staff.

Honour had not specified a time in her letter (yet another feature that made it all the more intriguing to him) but he expected that her carriage would arrive, at the latest, at some point between nine and ten o'clock in the evening. It would never do to arrive at a ball unfashionably early, but too late would be rude, after all. Before he knew it, seven o'clock had come and gone, and he was still gallivanting around his house in the same dusty clothes he had worn on the trip down from Nottinghamshire.

"Something appears to be occupying your mind this evening, sir", said Buckham, noncommittally, as he helped his master ease into his shirt. He then thought to add "- if you'll pardon the rather impertinent observation, that is."

"Yes Buckham, you are as perceptive as you ever were", Blackwood replied, too whimsically ebullient to even think of chastising his veteran manservant. "I do think I am rather distracted, but then, I have had rather a revelation over the last week. I will say no more for now, other than that having a sudden new perspective on one's life can do strange things to one's sense of composure."

"So they say, sir", said Buckham, as he forcefully pulled at Blackwood's top button.

"Oh Buckham," Blackwood could not help himself but continue, pleased to have this neutral and willing listener for his talk of the heart. "It is quite hopeless, I simply cannot take my mind off this. Perhaps I dare hope for more from my life than I have expected for many years."

"One hears of such a condition being common in those for whom something changes. Such as those who fall in love, sir."

Buckham raised a quizzical eyebrow at his master, unsure of how much information he might be able to draw out of him, but convinced that something very interesting indeed was happening.

"Yes, yes, I suppose one does. But then, I suppose that must indicate that this feeling is quite new to me, that I have never experienced it before. What a terrible shame, such an incomplete life I have led!"

"There is, as my father always maintained, a first time for everything, sir. If all things came to people with the ease of sight or breath, then life would contain no satisfaction and there would be little point in leading it at all."

Buckham walked purposefully to the other side of the room, fetched a bottle of *eau de cologne*, and applied a modest measure to a silk handkerchief.

"I never quite believed him as a younger man, of course. But then, like most youths, especially of the male sex, I was quite impatient, and wished for all things to come with both the qualities of immediacy, and ease. They do not, of course, but that is no reason to surrender to fatalism."

Buckham dabbed a little of the cologne onto Blackwood's wrist and the sides of his neck. The cold, wet sensation brought Blackwood back down to earth somewhat, reminding him of his temporal nature.

For a few moments he had been soaring with the angels on high, but now, Buckham's homely words and the splash of cologne on his neck had quite grounded him.

He inhaled the reassuringly familiar fresh, yet exotic, scent of citrus and sandalwood. The cologne was blended exclusively for him, the sandalwood oils brought back from one of his trips to the orient.

"Over time, I came to respect my father's simple advice more and more. When one has lived for many years as I have, one comes to realise that activities, which once brought one great difficulty, become quite simple as time progresses. Why, there was once a time when blacking a shoe was quite a challenge to me, but now I believe I could do rather a competent job even if I was blindfolded and had both hands tied behind my back. Ladies are of course, a rather more delicate concern than bootstraps, though I believe the same principle generally applies."

"Quite so Buckham, quite so. You really are a font of wisdom this evening, it is a shame I have not listened to your advice more assiduously in the past."

"Understandably sir, as you have very rarely sought it", said Buckham, a very slight edge to his voice, which Blackwood might almost have thought hinted at repressed humour. Buckham tucked a crisp silk handkerchief into Blackwood's pocket, a final touch.

He took great care and satisfaction in his master's sartorial elegance, which was, after all, reputed across all the great courts of the civilized world.

"- though I say it myself however, even one's servants have wisdom to impart, from time to time."

Buckham gave Blackwood what his master could have sworn was the slightest hint of a wink, and it took him great effort not to smile too warmly back at his valet – he felt that he had, perhaps, given Buckham quite enough shocks already for one evening.

"Indeed, Buckham. Best apply a double dose of cologne this evening."

"My pleasure, sir."

Chapter Eight

Honour was bored once again. Another ball, another set of frightfully dull suitors for her sister. She was sitting on the peripheries of another bespoke ballroom, listening to the same melodies being plonked out on a grand piano by some old maid who was approaching her bed time.

Beatrice was sipping at a heavily diluted punch while a fat-faced son of a Marquess did his best to be as charming and witty as the men in the novels his sister had probably read as they were growing up, while he was too busy with dogs and horses to even think about the impression he would one day make upon society.

"So, my Lady, do you hunt at all?"

The man brayed at her like a Sergeant-Major in the barrack house.

"Oh, oh dear", replied the pretty, timid girl who she'd been doing her best to show off to London society for the past month and a half. "- I am afraid I fear I have not, Mr. Delingpole."

"A terrible shame," he roared in response "- puts colour in your cheeks m'gal! A sound lass like you should come out to Hampshire and experience some country air! This nasty city stuff does one no good, bad for the lungs as well. My uncle Clovis got an awful hacking cough last year, after he had to spend a little time in London on business, hacked up half his lung all over his luncheon partridge! Haw haw! How we laughed, but all the stupid fault of passing one's life in this cesspit of a city, what?"

It was all Honour could do to suppress a cringe at this dreadful anecdote.

"Actually sir, this is my first time in London, I have spent most of my girlhood with my great aunt, in Bath."

"Bath, you say?" Mr Delingpole guffawed, causing him to spill a little of his ruby red wine onto his garish and overly decorated coat. To later be blamed on some long-suffering valet, no doubt, thought Honour with a little sigh. "I could never stand the godawful place! Not good for you, swilling down all that nasty water the Romans put there. How bloody long do you think that's been there girl? Centuries no doubt, and now they have the temerity to claim it's good for you. Stuff and nonsense I say, restorative properties my left buttock!"

Delingpole paused a moment, to fortify himself with another, rather inelegant, gulp of his wine, before continuing with his exposition on the subject of Bath.

"My cousin Toby got a terrible rash from taking the waters at Bath, as I hear is quite common, at least in aristocratic circles where peoples' skins are unused to the miasma of others! Had a nasty red rash all up and down his body which caused his skin to peel off all over the place! Nasty, but we did enjoy a good laugh at his expense! Haw haw!"

"If you say so, Mr. Delingpole, although I can personally see little to amuse in your unfortunate cousin's predicament. A skin condition is no laughing matter."

Honour sighed - there was no sight in heaven or earth more painful than watching a dim, humourless girl endure the conversation of a graceless oaf. The thought had no sooner come to Honour than she was off, sneaking away to another part of the room, safe in the knowledge that there was little need for any chaperone to come between the unhappy pair she left behind her.

For a moment, Honour found her eyes scanning the room, searching for James Blackwood, but then she remembered that his late arrival was her doing. She had deliberately sent a second carriage to fetch Mr Blackwood in order to leave him in some uncertainty as to her intentions, after having written him a note which might, she thought in retrospect, have led him to believe her perhaps more affectionate than she had intended. The second carriage was due to arrive precisely one hour after she and Beatrice had arrived in the first cortege, to allow her sister to settle into the ball a little away from the notorious rogue and seducer. Best to keep a fellow like Blackwood at arm's length, Honour had thought, and not give him too much of an inclination of one's possible affection for him too early.

She was, after all, not entirely certain herself of the depth of her feelings for him. She simply knew that seeing him again, no matter how she had tried to talk herself out of it, had become more desirable than avoiding him. However, there was no way that she was going to give him an advantage in this situation. A man with his experience could pounce like a cornered tiger if you weren't careful, as Lady Fenway had so eloquently put it.

Against what she had long presumed to be her better judgement, Honour had to admit that she had grown more than fond of Blackwood. There was something about him in their two most recent meetings, some strange combination of the mystique his reputation foreshadowed and which his proud, slightly weather-browned face bore witness to, and the vulnerability he had displayed before her, which reawakened what she had thought to be long discarded emotions.

His confession of his apparent feelings had been ill-judged and crude, it was true, and yet in the days since that strange afternoon in Fitzrovia the shadowy presence of Blackwood the cad, the dandy, the toast of all Europe's darkest bordellos had hung over her, stealing her sleep and prompting thoughts and notions of the man that she could not ignore. There had barely been any room for authentic attraction in her life, between her cossetted girlhood, a coquettish adolescence and the marriage she was bundled into at the age of nineteen, but now it was growing in her bosom and invading her bodily awareness in a way that no other attraction ever had. He was fascinating, this infamous villain who reserved a soft spot particularly for her, and she could not help but feel a tiny quiver of anticipation as she cast her eyes towards the clock and awaited the hour of his arrival.

And then, seemingly just as she realised that the clock was about to chime for ten o'clock, he stepped into the room, announced at once by a footman in a voice that did the drama of his reputation no justice.

"Mr James Blackwood." As ever, a hush fell on the room. Blackwood was quite used to this, but to Honour it seemed remarkable, a portent of things to come. She felt a rather shocking need to possess him, this man who silenced rooms with nothing but the announcement of his name, those sun touched cheeks, which spoke of exotic adventure, and that fine jawline, but she contained herself, remembered her position and the requirements of her sister, and became the first person in the room to successfully glance away in apparent indifference. Predictably enough, given that he was here as a result of her invitation, Blackwood came over.

"Baroness Fotherington" he purred, in that voice that had melted a thousand hearts before this one. "I must convey my gratitude. I had not known that it was a habit of yours to invite childhood acquaintances along to balls."

"Well might you thank me, Mr. Blackwood," she said with a tartness that she intended to convey all of the charged tension of the situation. She did not look him directly in the eye, compelling him to work for her affections now that the topic of her letter had been broached, if indirectly. "- it is, indeed, not a habit of mine, but was rather, on this occasion, an expression of cordiality. I have no wish to make an enemy of you." She could see Blackwood picking this over, internalising it, trying to reason out whether or not she was rebuffing him, or merely playing along with high society's usual formalities. She had him where she wanted him.

She had not played this game of social niceties cloaking complex desires for so long, really, not since her marriage, and found herself enjoying it to a rather surprising degree. Perhaps it was simply the man that she played with?

"Nor I of you, as I hope you have, by now, gathered", he spoke silkily, more composed than he had been on their previous two encounters. "- and by token of my gratitude, despite what your sister and others no doubt perceive as our advancing years, I should like to express such feelings by asking you to dance with me." Honour took her time to study him frankly. She looked him up and down, standing, feet somewhat apart and arms facing her, at his side. His eyes dilated slightly, and his chin gave the faintest tremble as she pondered her decision.

"Well" she said at last, in a calm tone that defused the tension, if only for a moment. "- I suppose that as a lady of my, as you so delicately phrased it yourself, 'advancing years' I ought to seize any opportunity that comes my way. I accept your gracious invitation, Mr. Blackwood." Blackwood beamed at her, smiling more fully than he had in years. She placed her hand in his, and fairly led him to the dance floor, so stunned was he by her prompt acceptance. Many eyes turned, whether envious of her, or a little disapproving of the sight of an ageing seducer and a recent widow taking so assertively to the floor she could not tell. Blackwood, regaining his usual composure around the fair sex, had assumed his posture, placed his hand firmly upon Lady Honour Northbrook, Baroness Fotherington's back, and begun to lead her in a well-executed waltz, all knew that this was not some strange stunt or perversion of decency, but rather a dance between old sweethearts, an expression of real closeness, and, despite everything, a rather sweet and seemly thing to behold.

Quite shockingly so – for, although James and Honour were, at that moment, completely oblivious to anything but each other, the gossips all over the room began to whisper in each other's ears, speculating on the meaning of it. They were rather unused to seeing James Blackwood dance with such obvious tenderness, holding his partner close, perhaps closer than propriety dictated, even for a waltz, and that partner not a woman known for her wild ways, nor a young chit that he hoped to seduce.

"You dance well for an old cad", Honour's voice was low, her words spoken close into Blackwood's ear. "Why, all of the young ladies looking on must rather envy me. I must confess this is a sensation I have not had for many years, to be watched and envied in this manner."

He took a moment to simply look at her, held there in his arms as they swirled elegantly around the floor. It seemed so improbable that they were here like this, that he felt almost certain that this was a dream, from which he would shortly awaken. She was, without question, quite the most beautiful woman that he had ever known, regardless of how many exotic beauties his travels had brought into his life. Tonight she positively glowed, dressed in a fashionable gown of delicate golds, all satin and lace, crystal and beads, highlighted by a sash that exactly set off her hair, and emphasised, with its placement, the creamy curves of her breasts as they were lifted on proud display by her corset.

It was the kind of dress that drew a man's eye to that shadowed valley between a lady's breasts, and his mind to thoughts of what lay just beneath the edge of the daring neckline.

Pulling his mind back to their conversation, James spoke lightly, teasingly, leaning his head down to bring his lips almost to her ear.

"As you have no doubt heard in salacious tea-room gossip…" he replied, growing in confidence, relishing the proximity of their two bodies. The closeness of his hips and thighs gave Honour a little tingling that passed on through her body and down her leg as she swayed from side to side, and a hotness in her breasts she had not experienced in a very long time. "… I have had many opportunities to practice my technique."

"Really?" said Honour, feigning innocence. "I should never have guessed, Mr. Blackwood. You are indeed, full of surprises." Blackwood recognised her irony, and allowed himself to laugh a little.

"I must concede that the vigour of this exercise has rather tired me. Would you accompany me onto the terrace for a moment's air?" At her nod of acquiescence, he guided their waltz to the edge of the floor, where they released each other, each with some regret, carefully concealed, came apart, and moved, politely through the crush, but as swiftly as possible, to the shadowed area near the doors to the terrace.

They stopped, concealed a moment by some artfully placed potted palms, and stared, for what felt like hours, into each other's eyes, his a rich brown, hers a stormy grey, lit by tiny silver flecks. Then, with a tiny nod from Honour and a knowing smile from Blackwood, they crept out through the French doors and into the London evening air.

Chapter Nine

Outside, the lights of Mayfair twinkled in the darkness.

The light of candles and gas-powered streetlights was just enough to illuminate the beautiful gardens which graced the rear of this magnificent house, well matched with the character of Grosvenor Square, which lay at the front of the house, with its manicured green and the little copse of trees at the centre, ringed by houses of pearly white. Everything in these fashionable parts of west London was so elegant, so clean, so well-maintained.

To think that opulence of this kind sat in a city side by side with immense poverty and squalor; the heaped horror of the rookeries in the east end and the putrid smudge of old father Thames flowing, oozing black and brown through the centre of it all was remarkable.

They were but feet from thousands of other lives entirely separate from their own, which were lived in different manners, according to different habits, customs and bank balances, and yet in a Square like this one, and a garden like this, so contained and perfect, so protected from the world, one could almost convince oneself that this was the whole world - wealthy, at ease with itself, and always on the verge of love.

The terrace was elegant, with carved marble balustrades, and urns, all filled with, or woven over with, huge swathes of hothouse roses and other blooms, brought in at great expense for the pleasure of the guests. Their delicate scents mingled on the air, threaded through with the subtle scent of the jasmine perfume that Honour wore.

"The air of London is fair tonight", remarked Blackwood softly, gazing up at the dramatic clouds drifting overhead. It was fairly late in the Season, and the weather was beginning to warm – the clouds might still presage rain, but for now it was still.

"Fairer than it often can be. I am used to the countryside of course", said Honour, maintaining a prim and practised composure.

"It is best to take the city these months, as the weather begins to warm, but when the oppressive heat of summer is not yet upon us", said Blackwood, "-words which can apply as much to London as to any other city. Streets are safer in the longer days, while the air is yet fresh, and ruffians have less taste for hard liquor and brawling."

"I shouldn't expect we shall encounter too much of that here in Grosvenor Square."

There was the undertone of a laugh in Honour's voice at the thought.

"Perhaps not, though complacency is rarely to be recommended in urban environs." He eyed her wolfishly, arching his back to pounce. "One never knows what one might find lurking in the shadows."

"Indeed?" said Honour, eyeing him once more with a playful air. "- and have you done much lurking in your time in the great metropolises of the earth, Mr. Blackwood?"

"More than a lifetime's worth."

Without either party being entirely conscious of it, they realised that, as they spoke, their faces had come close together, so that their lips were almost touching, and their eyes, dilated at the sight of the other, seemed to be linked by an unseen force, drawing them closer by the moment. Seconds ticked by like hours, a bird cried somewhere in the London night, and drawn by a force that neither felt able to, nor wished to resist, they kissed for the first time in eleven years.

James Blackwood was more used to kissing than he was to almost any other field of human endeavour. This time, though, was different. This time, there was an elemental flow to the whole thing, a collective seizing of the moment that took him entirely out of himself. His soul soared up towards heaven and the messy, physical detail of this embrace of bodies and lips and tongues, the exchange of pleasure taking place between them, whilst intense, seemed somehow unimportant. What mattered was the two of them, the feelings that they shared and the long emotional history brought now, at last, full circle, to a moment of unabashed shared connection.

The longing he felt for her was not crude lust that needed to be sated before it withered in his loins, but a steady, mellow sensation, a need to be close to this specific woman simply for the sake of it, simply because she was who she was. There was no other woman in the world he would even have acknowledged the existence of in that long, golden moment.

For Honour this was considerably newer than it was for Blackwood.

Her one fumbling and short lived affair with Rogers had not changed the fact that, to her, intimacy had always been an obligation, a duty that she had fulfilled for her family and her name, a gift that she had occasionally given to her old husband. She had never disliked him, but desire had not been a function of their relationship, at least not from her perspective. Their kisses had been dry and their touches, faltering and occasional. Now though, fires seemed to crackle within her, new sources of energy ignited by this old flame.

She remembered, now, basking in this new warmth of sensation, the few short kisses they had shared when she was nineteen, before they were torn apart by what she now saw as a terrible comedy of errors. She found that now, regardless of his reputation, or her long held opinions, she wished to give herself to him as fully as was humanly possible, in both body and spirit.

There were no comparisons she could make from her previous experience, and despite her age, this feeling of desire was almost entirely new to her. Could it be love? Was this the matured reality of what she thought she had felt, all those years ago?

"Now my Lady…", Blackwood whispered, breaking their communion at last, his breathing somewhat uneven, and his body hard with desire. She felt the lack of his lips on hers as a terrible loss, and leant into him, her head resting on his shoulder, as his arms still cradled her against him. "- I feel it would only be right for us to leave the younger bucks and lasses for whom this party has really been thrown, in peace."

"A most public-spirited suggestion, Mr. Blackwood" she whispered back. "- but where do you suggest we go?"

"We could take a Hansom cab back to my house in Mayfair?" he inquired without a moment's pause. "I am sure that someone can be found to attend to dear Beatrice, and ensure that she returns safely in your coach." Honour was astounded by his boldness, forgetting for a second the quality of experienced seducer she was dealing with here. "- I have ample spare space, as a bachelor, and many fines wines in the cellar. I'm sure you would be…" he eyed her lustily, a little of the old, notorious Blackwood, the rogue of high society, creeping back into the glint in his eyes. "… most comfortable."

Honour giggled at the dark humour in his voice, but then stopped herself. She realised fully, for the first time, how closely entwined their bodies had become, and though fully clothed and barely six feet from the main body of the ball there was an intense intimacy between them. They were holding each other, pressed against one another's bodies, each curve and softness of her body against the defined hard lines of his. Her heart hammered a new rhythm through her evening frock. She felt warm throughout, despite the light chill of the evening, and desired nothing more than to explore these sensations further – as fast as possible.

"I fear I must acquiesce to your request, Mr. Blackwood" she replied, her voice light, playful and almost girlish, her thoughts commanded now by the overpowering sensations in her body. All reason and caution had deserted her now.

"Lead on… Let us make arrangements for Beatrice's care post-haste, and be away."

It was not a long ride from Grosvenor Square to Blackwood's house, and there was no traffic to impede their progress. The cabbie, a bluff old cockney of the sort one expects to find at the reins of a London cab, did not ask any probing questions – they had money, and it was not his place to enquire. Most likely he assumed that they were a long married upper-class couple who had grown tired of society's formalities and wished to return home, leaving the coach that they had arrived in for others in their party. In making such an assumption he would not have been correct, but not completely wrong either.

Honour was content to leave Beatrice for a while. She had not reasoned out the implications of her liaison on her sister's evening, but she could be confident that as long as the ball went on, Beatrice would be quite safe and well, under the watchful eyes of her hosts.

Most of the young gentlemen present were too charmless and dim to pose any real threat to her.

Beatrice had been all too ready to stay and enjoy herself, when Honour had claimed a return of her megrim, and assured Beatrice that Mr Blackwood would see her home safely, so that the coach could remain for Beatrice. Indeed, as far as gentlemen were concerned, the only true potential menace to Beatrice, present at the entire party, was right next to her, clasping her hand in his and making her feel flushed and shivering with desire, just at his touch, as they sped through the streets towards his infamous den. She had neutralised any threat James Blackwood might pose to her family's honour by absorbing his advances herself, she thought with a smile.

On arriving, Blackwood was pleased to note that Stanford seemed to have taken the liberty of tidying the drawing room. This being the house of a hard-living bachelor, it was rarely in a fit state to entertain any guests other than Blackwood's own circle of rogues and dandies, who were less inclined to notice the stains of spilled port, or the lingering smell of cigar ash. Stanford and the staff did try to maintain a standard regardless, but, he had to confess, he had been in the habit of making it very hard for them. On this particular occasion however, the house was smart and did its owner credit. There was no musky, manly smell of indulgent evenings, no cracked glasses or piles of unloved clutter. The place was as it should be, elegant, respectable and urbane.

Honour barely registered the house, beyond it pleasing lack of any other persons, and the fact that the delightful, and rather exotic scent that James wore as cologne seemed to pervade the house as well.

It was a scent that she found both soothing and arousing. There was a moment, as the door closed behind them, when she wondered what she was doing here, but she pushed the thought firmly aside.

Her heart was beating hard, her breath was uneven and she felt more completely out of control than she ever had in her life. And she found that she didn't care.

James led her through the door of the drawing room, flicked the door closed behind them, and stopped, looking at her with eyes lit with desire. For a moment she felt self-conscious, unsure of what she was doing, then all doubts were swept aside as he pulled her into his arms.

Falling, almost as a single entity, onto a conveniently sited couch, they resumed the passionate kissing which had been, perforce, interrupted by their travel here. This time the moment was not soft and sweet but hard, with two bodies pressing into each other lustily. All of the repressed longing, desire, guilt and frustration of eleven years was expressed in the intensity of their connection.

Honour had made this decision and now she was eager to see it to its fruition, abandoning herself to Blackwood's dark, slender fingers and his seducers' talents. She wanted to wipe all memory of past hurt from his mind, to bring them together as it should have been in the beginning, had either of them been able to see the truth.

Without entirely knowing what she was doing, some instinct compelled her hands and fingers to explore his body, taking in his arms and chest and thighs with a profound fascination.

She was only used to the podgy body of an ailing baron in the boudoir, and Blackwood, despite being almost past his physical prime, was a far more compelling specimen. She could feel the strength of his arms, the firmness of his upper legs, and the hard definition of his chest as her fingers softly pulled at the edges of his coat and shirt while he scattered kisses on her neck and brought her up panting and shaking.

She could sense pleasure creeping in, a storm of intense feeling brewing in her breasts and beneath her widow's petticoats. It startled her, that she should feel such intensity just from his kisses – nothing in her experience had led her to think such a thing possible.

In a rush of frantic activity, through which he somehow managed to never stop kissing her, his jacket was off, his shirt undone, his cravat tossed to the side, and then all finally abandoned to the shining parquet floor. He laid himself on the finely-upholstered couch, pulling her to him, a paler body revealed under his linen shirts, less harsh and sun-browned than his face, yet still firm and muscular. She had unpicked his outer defences and the real Blackwood was now revealed, the one hidden from the prying eyes of society.

She found him beautiful, in the clean lines of his body and the sudden vulnerability in his eyes, which came with his near nakedness. She wrapped herself close to him, running her hands over his naked skin, and sliding her body against his. Her skirts were somehow pulled up and she found herself almost astride his body, her most intimate parts pressed against the hardness of his cock, with only the thin layer of his breeches between them.

The sensation was exquisite, and the experience aroused, within her, passions she had thought long buried by years of marriage and domestic tedium.

She ran her lips over his chest and shoulder, tasting her way up to his neck, as his clever fingers worked at the delicate buttons on the back of her dress, releasing them one by one. The cool air reached her heated skin as he did so, making her shiver with the sensation.

Lifting her effortlessly, he pulled her higher, and eased the bodice of the dress down, to expose her breasts to his clever tongue. Honour gasped at the sensation as he suckled first one nipple then the other, making jolts of sheer pleasure spark straight from her breasts, to deep between her legs.

She did not even notice his fingers working at unlacing her corset, until the cool air again touched skin that was rarely exposed. Pausing in his kisses for a moment, he lifted her up, so that she sat, poised, her full weight pressing her down upon his aching cock. She moaned at the sensation, for the first time in her life actively wanting a man inside her, and helped him pull her dress, stays and chemise off, leaving her also naked from the waist up. He untied the strings of her petticoats, and pulled those up over her head also.

His hands explored her body, the soft curve of her back, the pinkness of her nipples standing now hard and upright, and the languid stretch of her stomach all revealed. He held her and she was conscious of her own skin as it tingled, her breasts as he kissed them emphatically and they smouldered with the heat of his passion, feeling swollen and more sensitive than ever before.

A new open, hot wet feeling was growing ever more intense down below, where their most intimate and vulnerable areas seemed to be pressing ever closer to one another.

Unable to bear the existence of any fabric between them a moment longer, she pushed herself up and stood, just long enough to pull off her drawers, standing, luxuriating in the sensation of being completely naked for a moment, before bending her attention to undoing his falls. His fingers came to help her, and soon he was released, his manhood standing proud before her.

It was impressive – certainly more so than her husband's had ever been. The sight aroused her, made the ache between her legs intensify, and she licked her lips unconsciously at the thought. The sight of that brought a groan to his lips, and he went to move, then groaned again, in frustration, his breeches trapped by his boots, which were, unfortunately, still on his feet. Seeing his predicament, Honour laughed, and leant to help him remove the offending boots, so that he could remove his breeches. The sight of her delightful buttocks, as she bent to pull on the boots was almost too much for him, and he bit his lip in an agony of desire.

Finally released from the last of his clothes, he drew her to him again, she coming willingly into his arms, to a passionate kiss as he drew her up against him, her body lying over his on the couch, and then, exquisitely, torturously slowly, he slid her back down again, sliding into her as he did. She gasped his name as he entered her, arching her back so that her breasts were thrust against his mouth, and he took full advantage of that movement, suckling and kissing until she cried out in pleasure, squirming on him in response.

It took every bit of control that he could muster, not to simply spend himself at that moment, so intense was the physical and emotional pleasure.

He had, he realised, dreamed this, many, many nights of the last eleven years, forcing all memory of those dreams aside until now. This was a consummation of more than lust, more than love, it was a consummation of years of the tragedy of love thought lost, played out now upon this soft red sofa in a west London townhouse, a location that could as easily have been anywhere on earth.

They began to move together, finding each other's rhythm, throbbing hardness enclosed in moist softness, boldly thrusting against each other, into the other's intimate space, penetrating each other's heart and soul as much as joining bodily. He held her close and gently bit her neck, and Honour threw her proud, red gold mane back, elegant coiffure ruined, pins fallen and tangles of hair drifting to caress his skin, in a moment of ecstatic satisfaction.

James was momentarily aware, before the pleasure overrode all conscious thought, of the concept that, with Honour, this was different – he felt no need to dominate or control, no need for anything but this deep and intense sharing of pleasure.

Part of him looked back at himself, at the incident with Blanchette, and other seductions, and did not know that man. It was not him – this, the way that he was with Honour, this was truly him. He let the reality of Honour wash the last of those memories away.

She found herself moving on him faster, driven by some unknown need inside her, recognising that there was so much more to this coupling of man and woman than she had ever touched on with Fotherington, and reaching for that completion. This was life, she thought, as it is intended to be lived.

This is love as it should be made, a feeling that is worth pursuing and waiting for and then finally, accepting. He matched his movements to hers, the pace accelerating and each thrust driven by years lost and desire, long repressed, now released.

He shuddered, she gasped for air, almost forgetting to be breath as she was consumed by passion, and then finally, they reached a mutual crest on their wave of passion, and shattered, crying out each other's names, as pleasure overwhelmed them.

Neither knew how long it was before they came back to a sense of themselves, still tangled in each other's arms. To begin with, there were no words. They simply drank each other in, watching the emotions bared in the other's eyes, knowing that there was much to be said, but with no idea at all where to start.

Eventually, tentatively, Honour brought her finger to trace the line of his jaw, to drift across his lips, wondering at the joy of being able to touch him.

James kissed her fingertips as they brushed his lips, and smiled, as amazed at the moment as she was. He felt something that he had never felt before, he realised. He felt loved.

It was terrifying, it was beautiful, he wanted to stay in this moment forever, lest this slip from his grasp and leave him back in the darkness that had been his life for eleven years. But they could not stop time. He needed to say something.

"We should have done that eleven years ago", said Blackwood, and they both laughed a moment as they tried to find how to go on together, now that everything had changed.

"Perhaps..." said Honour, coyly. As the pleasurable haze faded however, she could feel herself realising who and where she was once again.

She was conscious of having left Beatrice behind, of her filial duties, of her deceased husband.

She was certainly attracted to James Blackwood it was true, but suddenly there were so many questions, so much complexity. And, she realised in a moment of cold shock, he had just said that they should have been intimate eleven years ago, not that he should have married her, or that he loved her. She rose to her feet and started to dress, to reassemble the tangle of clothing into something in which she could be seen.

"What are you doing?" said Blackwood, who had turned to collect his clothing from the floor, then turned back, still naked, to see her struggling to tighten her corset laces herself. A look of confusion and panic came over him, and Honour was assailed by a desire to give him comfort. She resisted though, set already on her course.

"I'm sorry Mr. Blackwood... James, but I have responsibilities..." she pulled the dress on, concealing her body from him.

Sternly she bade her nipples return to their normal state, and her body to cease the sensations of arousal. Her body rebelliously disobeyed, but she was not going to let him see that.

"- I have a younger sister to look out for and a family reputation to maintain. I must return at once to my home, so that I am there when Beatrice returns. Whatever will she think if I am not! Farewell."

She slipped her shoes on and fairly ran back out into the London night, leaving Blackwood to dress himself, feeling abandoned, and afraid. He had just found her again, just been given a taste of the paradise that could be his, with her beside him, and now he was once more alone. What if she regretted this night? What if she would not see him again? He could not imagine, after this, spending the rest of his life with anyone but her.

His thoughts stilled – that was exactly what he wanted, it came to him in a moment of clarity – he wanted to spend the rest of his life with Honour – married to her.

He needed a brandy. He was terrified, he could not lose her again.

Chapter Eleven

Blackwood awoke the next day with a headache. Once again he had felt the need to drink too much liquor to ease the pain in his heart, and once again the following morning he had woken with a skull-splitting pain in his head. His bowels were unsettled and he felt a strong desire never to eat, fraternise or drink ever again. Well after one in the afternoon, Buckham came in with a silver tray of coffee and some breakfast, pulling aside the curtains to allow the excessively bright light of day to intrude into his master's darkness.

"I have prepared a restorative breakfast, sir."

"Thank you Buckham." Blackwood muttered from under the covers, still half asleep. The bright light of this late July morning was not a welcome intruder, but the smell of coffee did arouse a small desire to do more than lounge beneath his bedsheets.

"Your efforts are not unappreciated old boy", Blackwood continued, still bed-bound. "Nevertheless, I fear that they are in vain. Dead men need no sustenance, and, beyond the lingering of my physical self, after last night's exertions I find I am, to all intents and purposes, deceased."

"That seems a rather premature conclusion, if I might be so bold sir." Buckham replied, his servant's façade not cracking for an instant in the face of his employer's melodramatic pronouncements. "I hope sir is not planning on anything too hasty?" he added, gesturing to the loaded flintlock pistol Blackwood was in the habit of keeping next to his bed. It was permanently at full cock, and could be let off at the slightest provocation.

Ever since a harrowing incident in Gibraltar, when Blackwood had been dragged from his bed in the small hours of the morning by a pair of local rogues who were looking to rob him, he had considered this a necessary security measure. Rumours about why he kept a firearm to hand even as he slept had only added to his legend in fashionable London circles.

"Good God man! I'd never dream of it!" blustered Blackwood with renewed energy, as he realised what his manservant was suggesting. Blackwood had never been that deeply the self-indulgent type, and had usually brushed personal crises aside with ease. This time however, he felt an unfamiliar urge to wallow in self-pity, of the type that he had not felt since he was but a boy.

"Most reassuring, sir."

"Don't be absurd Buckham! I would have hoped that you would know me better than that by now!"

"If I might risk adding to your present predicament sir, I find it is best not to be complacent where affairs of the heart are concerned." On the last words, the old valet's inflection rose a little, and he leaned forward to indicate to Blackwood that he was perfectly aware of what was going on. Blackwood sighed, of course he was! Buckham was the canniest man in all of London, he knew everything that went on under this roof, and though he had the good sense to keep quiet about it, probably had insights to share on all manner of delicate subjects.

"Oh, Buckham, I fear that you are quite right. You have seen right into my soul. I yearn for her, and yet it seems she has spurned me once again. Soon she will return to the countryside and all will be lost." At this, Buckham gave a wry smile, and placed a cup of fresh coffee on the bedside table.

"Then I suppose it is up to sir to decide on a course of action", he said.

"What do you mean, Buckham?"

"Well, I suppose if sir is quite content to live the rest of his life haunted by an unsatisfied longing and hypothetical questions then that is sir's business. If however, sir seeks answers to the dilemma rending his very soul, then it falls to sir to affect some clarification of his feelings, for better or for worse. It is no use passing the rest of our days pondering what might have been; it falls to us every once in a while to establish certainty, or else give up altogether."

Blackwood mulled this pronouncement over, sipped some coffee, and considered his position. Then like a flash of lightning ' breaking the monotony of a warm summer's day, an idea came to him.

He had never been more convinced of anything in all of his life. The path he must take was now laid out before him. He sprang from bed, scalded his throat tossing back the remainder of the coffee in one gulp, and presented himself, near naked but entirely unashamed, to his faithful servant.

"Dress me, Buckham", he declared, holding out his arms with renewed vigour and purpose. "Dress me as swiftly as you dare."

"As sir desires." Buckham gave a little bow, and a hint of a wink, heading towards the wardrobe, and a selection of finely tailored shirts.

Chapter Twelve

Honour sat in her drawing room, staring out the window, not seeing what was out there, but only her own thoughts. She had barely slept. Thankfully, she had been ensconced here, as if she had never been anywhere else, when Beatrice was delivered home. All that she had wanted to do was think, to try to sort out her tangled emotions, to relive the amazing sensations that still sent shivers of pleasure through her body, and to decide what all of that meant, for her future.

It was a forlorn hope. Beatrice had wittered on for two hours, about every gentleman that she had spoken to (they were all, still totally unsuitable – Honour began to despair), who she had danced with, and all the gossip from the other girls. By the end of it, Honour had the beginnings of a real megrim, and took the excuse of her megrim 'returning' to escape to bed, with a posset to soothe her.

Sleep did not oblige. Provided an interminable number of hours to sit and think, as a result of being unable to sleep, she had half driven herself mad, reliving the evening in her mind, over and over again.

There was no doubt that her body craved the physical pleasure that she now knew James could give her, a pleasure so much greater than she had ever imagined, indeed she had become heated and sensitive of skin just thinking about it.

There was also no doubt, she was ashamed to admit to herself, that she had, just like a silly young chit, fallen helplessly in love with the man. Again. One would think that having one's heart broken by the man once would be enough. But no, here she was, setting herself up for that to happen all over again. The words that he had spoken, breaking the spell of the amazing pleasure that they had shared, came back to her, with terrible clarity.

"We should have done that eleven years ago."

Nothing about love, nothing about marriage, nothing but a sadly off-colour reference to a callow young man's desire to have her physically. She was close to tears, thinking of it. But she was of a practical turn of mind. She would not lie to herself. If last night was all that she ever had of James, she would treasure it – she would not regret such a magnificent experience.

But she wanted more. She wanted, foolish though it was to even consider, from the most notorious rake of this generation, to spend the rest of her life with him. She wanted to be his wife. There, she had thought the words.

Thinking them did not make it any more likely. This time the tears did come – they were tears of regret – for her foolishness eleven years ago, for the sad, wasted nature of those eleven years, and for the endless, desolate years that she could see ahead of her, if she could not have James.

And it seemed unlikely that she could. He would, having now added her to his list of successful seductions, cast her aside, go in search of some younger, prettier woman to seduce, and leave her to heartbreak again.

She was quite aware that lack of sleep was making her rather melodramatically maudlin, but, defiantly, she let herself wallow in it for a time. Clearly, her 'oh so brilliant idea' of inviting him to that ball, and encouraging his attentions, had been abysmally bad judgement on her part. Yet, even now, she could not regret it. The memory of his kisses, of his body moving with hers, was delicious, and would have to be enough to keep her warm through the years ahead.

Still, she let herself imagine, just for a little, what it would be like if James came to her, if he forgave her hard words and hasty retreat, if he loved her, as he had implied, all those days ago, at Lady Fenway's. She would, she decided, throw all propriety to the winds, should he come to her. She would tell him her feelings, risk everything to hope that he might reciprocate them, before she accepted that all hope was lost.

Having reached that conclusion, she finally drifted into sleep, tossing and turning, dreaming strange dreams of physical passion and loss, until Jane came to wake her in the late morning, to ready her for the day.

And now, she had dressed plainly, performed a minimal toilette, broken her fast – not eating, much, as today it tasted rather like sawdust – and seated herself here. Supposedly to embroider, but the work lay untouched in her lap, and she stared unseeing out the window.

And the thoughts went around in her head, all over again. She almost wished that Beatrice would rise, and launch into conversation, which would demand a response from her, just to provide a distraction. She wondered, self-pitying for a moment, how long it would take her to accept that James would never appear on her doorstep with declarations of love.

She had a nasty suspicion that the answer was…. forever.

Chapter Thirteen

"Faster driver, faster!" Blackwood yelled, holding his head out of the window of the carriage as they sped through the streets of London. They were careening rapidly towards Kensington, where he had heard Honour and her young sister were staying, in the city house that her late husband had bequeathed her.

Blackwood had thrown all caution out with the cigar smoke-tainted remains of last night's whisky. Leaning out, his head almost struck the edge of a fish merchants stand, earning cries of anguish from the surrounding crowd. He did not care, personal safety and his dignity before the masses had never been great preoccupations of James Blackwood, and now, consumed by his mission and the love that had sat, growing in his heart for all of eleven years, he cared even less.

"They're going as fast as their hindquarters can carry 'em, good sir!" yelled the cabbie over the noise of cobbled streets. His head was entirely bald, and his voice a thick east-end drawl. "If I apply the lash any more firmly, I fear they shall collapse on me and we shall both be thrown clear!"

"Damn it all man! Give the blighters everything you've got! Should we make it before one o'clock there's a guinea in it for you!"

"Very good sir!" said the cabbie, clearly motivated to renewed feats of speed by the offer of a fortnight's wages. The cab sped on, seeming to gain some significant speed as the driver's crack forced the agile black cab horses, from canter ever closer to a gallop.

Sweat accumulated between Blackwood's fingers, the anticipation was all too much. He longed only to be at his destination, at Honour's side, gaining the answers he had long sought.

With an abrupt heave that almost threw him from his seat, the cab pulled up at the side of a well-to-do looking West London street.

"Here we are sir, Bellevue Avenue, as requested."

"Thank you my man", said Blackwood, fairly wrenching open the door. "- and as a man of my word, I would be very happy to recompense you in full..." swiftly rummaging in his pockets, Blackwood presented his driver with two large gold coins. The man accepted, grinningly, and pulled away to find his next client.

Blackwood paused for a moment before tapping the front door with his fist. There was no denying it, this was one of the most significant moments of his life, and was not to be undertaken lightly. A small shiver ran down his back, unsettling his collar and his perfectly coiffed hair. "Faint heart never won fair maid", he whispered to himself, so quietly that it was barely a passing breath on the breeze. His father had said that to him, once upon a time, when his wild oats had yet to be sown and women still seemed like ethereal creatures, goddess-like in their distance and stature. *'Faint heart never won fair maid'* his thoughts repeated as his fingers tapped thrice and he waited as long as was needed.

A small part of Blackwood was relieved when a servant answered. The man was short and rotund, with a pair of brass pince-nez, which looked desperately in need of a polish, perched on a round, red nose.

"Can I help you at all?" he asked in a donnish manner, clearly confused by this stranger's presence on the doorstep.

"Yes, my good man," Blackwood replied "- might I enquire as to the whereabouts of Baroness Fotherington?"

"She is present, here in the household," the man said, eyeing him suspiciously. "Might I ask, sir, do you have an appointment, with my lady?"

"I'm afraid not, but I am here on very urgent business, and I think…"

"I'm sorry sir, I cannot simply let you in without an appointment. I shall enquire within, thank you for your patience…" and with that the door was shut softly but firmly in James Blackwood's face.

Perhaps unsurprisingly, this was enough to trigger a further crisis within Blackwood. What on earth was going on? Was Honour present, and if so, would she see him?

Was it possible that he had been too hasty the previous evening, that she had had a sudden change of heart, once the blinkers of momentary lust had been removed, and had decided to move on from their short-lived affair entirely? Could she even have instructed her servants to bar him from her presence, was she now behind the door, anxiously waiting for him to leave her in peace?

Moments ticked by, Blackwood could feel himself shivering, and all of his life seemed at once to converge on this one moment, this fleeting instant here on the doorstep, awaiting the verdict of the woman he now knew to be the love of his life.

Moments became minutes, and stretched to what felt like hours, until James was forced to believe that all was lost, that she would not see him, did not care for him, that he was the worst kind of fool. The despairing thoughts rolled around in his head, and, shoulders drooping, he turned, intending to leave, to drown his sorrows in brandy yet again. Just as he began to turn, raising his arm to hail a cab, to ferry him at once from this, the scene of his final humiliation, Honour opened the door.

"James", she said, in a tone that was concerned, but friendly, although, he noticed, her voice shook a little. "This is most unexpected."

"Indeed", he responded, struck, for a moment, by her appearance.

Even now, wearing a quite plain day dress in light yellow and with her face unmade, her beautiful hair pulled back into a simple knot, she radiated beauty and vitality like seemingly no other woman on earth. "I trust you arrived here before young Beatrice, without incident, yesterday evening?"

"Yes, yes she was quite alright in the end. She barely noticed I'd gone, really, and when she got home, and discovered that I was quite recovered from my 'megrim', all she could do was chatter on about her evening. Oh James," her voice shook badly on his name, and Honour reached out for his hand, to draw him in through the door, straight into her arms. She held him close to her and he could feel her quivering in his arms, as if with fear of something. Once his second of shock had passed, Blackwood was more than pleased to press Honour closer to him, concerned at her shakiness. He was determined, though, he would not let that distract him from his purpose – he had to do this before he lost his nerve completely.

"I'm so glad you came, I felt perfectly beastly abandoning you the way that I did, but you must understand, I have a young sister to care for." Her voice was a little too high, a little brittle, but her eyes shone as she looked at him.

"Yes", Blackwood said. "I quite understand. And I am glad, of course, that you are glad, for there was something I wanted to say to you, Honour." It was the first time he had felt entitled to use her Christian name since they were little more than children. (Apart that was, he corrected himself in his thoughts, from when he called out her name at the point of that quite magnificent completion last night.)

"Pray sir, and what is that?"

Blackwood took a deep breath, stepped back from the lady he now knew, without any doubt, he loved, and braced himself for the greatest adventure of his life.

"Honour, I know that you are still coming to terms with the loss of Baron Fotherington, and I know that to you I must seem a rather rough and coarse fellow, but truly, you inspire passions in me, of the heart, not just the body, which I did not think myself capable of experiencing. Truly, I love you, my Lady. I have loved you all these past eleven years, no matter what I did to try to stop that from being the case. If you feel any true affection for me, or, dare I hope, love, then I ask you to make me the happiest man in London, nay, all the world, by agreeing to be my bride."

On the final word, he fairly threw himself onto one knee, ignoring the painful result of slamming his knee into unforgiving marble. He stared up into Honour's eyes, and could see the glitter of the first traces of tears forming in them. She smiled at him, and in a shaky, but happy, voice said.

"Of course I will James. Why, I thought you'd never ask."

Little did James know how literal those words were, and Honour was not about to tell him – not yet, anyway.

Rising to his feet, James Blackwood, formerly the most scandalous seducer in Europe, soundly kissed his bride-to-be and was happy to be alive.

Three months later, as the summer began to fade, so too did the gossip. For there had been quite a remarkable amount of gossip. That James Blackwood, notorious rake, and breaker of hearts should have chosen to marry was astounding, that he had done so for love was beyond all belief to the jaded denizens of the *ton*. Bets had been taken, that he would call it off at the last moment, or that she would leave him, once she truly understood the scope of his iniquity.

The betting books at Whites were full of his name, all through the summer, and large sums changed hands as a result. James had ignored it all, much as he always had the reports of his more disreputable exploits, when they were splashed across the dailies. He was much too happy, spending his days with Honour – after all, they had eleven years to make up for!

Perhaps the most shocked of all had been Beatrice, who, in her rather naive and innocent way, had been so caught up in her own concerns, so flattered by the attention of multiple gentlemen, that she had barely noticed her sister's increasing preoccupation, and distractedness.

They had married in some haste, unable to bear waiting, now that they had uncovered each other's long held passion.

Beatrice's shock soon turned to joy, with the prospect of a romantic wedding, between two who were so obviously in love. James had weathered a rather excessive level of ragging from his closest friends, who found themselves having difficulty accepting the change in him.

Nonetheless, Travers had agreed to stand up with him, and had offered, with the assistance of his younger brother, to host the wedding breakfast at his very large London residence.

Honour found it darkly amusing that they had, somehow, become 'the wedding of the season', because, she suspected, no one could bear to stay away, if only to see who won the bets, about whether they would go through with it or not.

Now, remembering, sitting in her drawing room, James at her side, she smiled as the late summer sunshine lit golden drifts of fine dust motes in the air, gilding Beatrice's normally flat dark blonde hair to sparkling highlights. Beatrice was looking flushed, and rather beautiful today, with all of her attention focused on the conversation of her companion.

Nash Harringdon, Viscount Challoner, was the Marquess of Travers younger brother, and currently the heir to his title.

Should Travers ever marry, that might change, of course, but, even with the example of Blackwood before him, Travers still swore that he would never marry.

Nash and Beatrice had met at James and Honour's wedding, and taken to each other at first sight. To Honour's relief, Viscount Challoner was everything that Travers was not – he was quiet, not prone to the rakish behaviour of his brother, yet not timid or dull – he cared a great deal for the estates that Travers left to his care, and was, rather effectively, restoring the fortunes that his brother had spent.

Finally, Beatrice had a suitor who was completely acceptable. It was early days yet, but Honour could hope! Hope for a love for Beatrice to match what she had with James.

She turned to James, to find him watching her, as she had been watching Beatrice, his dark eyes full of love, and a promise of passion to come. She smiled, her love for him lighting up her face, and leant to let her head rest on his shoulder, content, truly content, for the first time in her life.

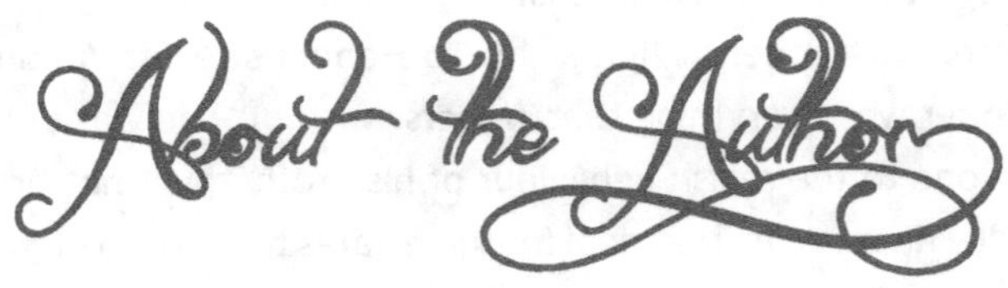

Arietta Richmond has been a compulsive reader and writer all her life. Whilst her reading has covered an enormous range of topics, history has always fascinated her, and historical novels been amongst her favourite reading.

She has written a wide range of work, from business articles and other non-fiction works (published under a pen name) but fiction has always been a major part of her life. Now, her Regency Historical Romance books are finally being released. The Derbyshire Set is comprised of 10 shorter novels (6 released so far). The 'His Majesty's Hounds' series is comprised of 10 novels, with the fifth having just been released.

She also has a standalone longer novel shortly to be released, and two other series of novels in development.

She lives in Australia, and when not reading or writing, likes to travel, and to see in person the places where history happened.

Be the first to know about it when Arietta's next book is released!

Sign up to Arietta's newsletter at

http://www.ariettarichmond.com

When you do, you will receive a free copy of the subscriber exclusive novella **'A Gift of Love',** a prequel to the Derbyshire Set series, which ends on the day that 'The Earl's Unexpected Bride' begins

This story is not for sale anywhere – it is absolutely exclusive to newsletter subscribers!

Other Books in 'The Derbyshire Set'

Available at all good book stores and for ebook readers too!

Coming Soon!

(You'll find a taste of Book 6 over the page !)

Here is your preview of the next book in 'The Derbyshire Set' by Arietta Richmond

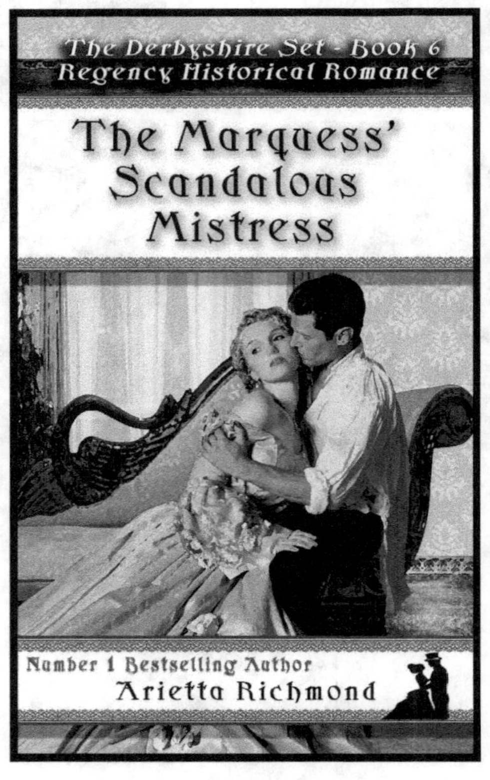

The Derbyshire Set ~ Book 6
Regency Historical Romance

The Marquess Scandalous Mistress

Arietta Richmond

Chapter One

"Well" said Lady Olivia Asterwood, Marchioness Hemsbridge, her voice becoming somewhat shrill, a reflection of the intense frustration that she was repressing, "- you're going to have to find a wife sometime, Sterling my boy, you're thirty now, after all, and tonight should present as good an opportunity as any."

"Yes mother, indeed it shall" replied her son, Sterling Asterwood, Marquess Hemsbridge, in a voice which was flat and lacking any conviction.

This was a speech that he had heard so often he could probably have quoted it verbatim if requested. Since he'd been barely out of swaddling clothes and away from his nanny's bosom his mother had been pressing him towards the skirt-hems of young ladies, whispering 'matrimony' from afar, without the barest hint of subtlety.

It was her obsession, her *raison d'etre,* her first vague notion in the morning sunlight and her final quivering half-thought before sleep. She was obsessed with maintaining their bloodline, and with the genealogy of the aristocracy in general.

"I simply can't understand it Sterling" she rambled on, undeterred by his outward lack of interest. "We never had any of these difficulties with Tobias, or Gloriana for that matter.

Both your siblings managed to fall into suitable matches in no time at all, yet that achievement seems to have defeated you. And you being the eldest everyone expected you to do your duty first. Most peculiar, I'm afraid to say, it's the talk of the county balls."

"I don't give a jot what they say at your blasted balls mother!" Sterling snapped back. "This is my own life and, at present, I am quite satisfied with the liberties of bachelorhood." It was only half a lie.

Of course the Marquess of Hemsbridge wanted a Marchioness, eventually. Of course he woke up in the mornings wishing the cold pillow beside him was supporting the warmth of a pretty young head.

Of course he pursued women, girls, ladies, pretty, plain all manner of women at the balls he managed to get to without his mildly outrageous mother in tow, and he certainly achieved some pleasant results from his pursuit.

Just not the sort of results that he wished to share with his mother, nor the sort that ever seemed to lead to the ringing sound of wedding bells.

"It's not that you aren't handsome, my boy," said the Marchioness, pinching his cheek in what she mistakenly believed to be an affectionate gesture (it had ceased to be so when he was about six…), "handsome and charming to boot, with feet that can dance and a tongue that can talk. Too picky is what you are, picky as a Reverend with an upset stomach, as my nanny used to say. Lord knows what she meant, but you shouldn't take that attitude about me, or Somerset society for that matter. If you want to make your way out of the Doldrums of bachelorhood and into the sweet harbour of marriage, you shall have to depend on both."

"Yes mother, as you wish" Hemsbridge ran his fingers through his lush copper brown hair, only to find a knot which he could not seem to push through. The effort hurt, but his mother did not notice his grimace of pain.

"Why I must say…" she blurted, after sipping the last of her afternoon tea. She was rather enjoying herself, sitting in the drawing room, supping at sweet, milky tea and lecturing her son. "… had I been as picky as you are, Sterling, when I was in my twenties, I'd never have married your father, oh good god no! He was a right clodhopper, with two left feet and no conversation whatsoever. But still, he was handsome enough, and had a fortune that was at least commensurate with my dynastic expectations, and that was that. I did what was to be done, for my family name, and for my unborn infants. And now here you are."

"Your generosity does you credit, my lady." Hemsbridge muttered sarcastically. At times like this, a small part of him wished she'd never bothered.

"Duty my boy, duty, that's the most important thing. It matters more than anything. More than any pretty face, or well-cut dress, or a successful afternoon's cavorting at the Derby. Duty to one's family, to one's future, to one's ancestors, to what went before and what is still to come. Without a firm commitment to duty, you shall die not only lonely, but also without issue, and more than just you shall be dead, Sterling Asterwood, your family will die too. The great coat of arms emblazoned on your doorway, the rich blue blood that flows in your veins, the name that you were born too, all will cease to be. Never forget it, it is all infinitely more important than any paltry rot you read in books about love, and romance. Those things are all well and good when you're young and have no commitments, but in time, one must realise what is important, and keep the good ship Hemsbridge afloat."

"Most insightful mother. Aristotle, I feel, could not have put it better. But now, if you'll excuse me, I have pheasants to be shooting." He rose to his feet rapidly, but was quickly returned to the embrace of the plump armchair he'd been occupying by his mother's stick. She flicked it up at him with an agility that defied the concept that she needed to use it, which indeed she did not – it was an affectation on her part - and used it to prod him back to a seated position.

"Oh no, you will not be shooting pheasant this afternoon, my good Marquess Hemsbridge!" she declared, emboldened by his look of confusion. "There is another sort of bird entirely you shall be hunting tonight, at the Duke of Whitehaven's ball. You shall eschew the cheap thrills of the chase for the hunting of another breed of prey entirely: a suitable wife!"

Hemsbridge rolled his eyes, considered protesting or running away, declined to bother with either, and resigned himself to another night of stilted conservation amongst Somerset society, in the presence of his dearly beloved mother.

"Ooh, that's Lady Arianna Betstaff!" exclaimed the Marchioness Hemsbridge, between mouthfuls of ratafia.

"Wonderful match, don't you think, such an eligible young lady. Her roots go deep, all the way back to William the Conqueror I hear. She's the talk of the West Country."

"Is she indeed?" Hemsbridge mumbled. He glanced over at the young lady but was not deeply impressed. She had a face that was too round, like a dinner plate someone had decorated with a muddy blonde wig. Her demeanour and mannerisms gave her the look of a girl who spends a bit too much time laughing along with men's jokes and presuming friendship, a trait that he had never found attractive.

"That girl behind her is at least as eligible too!" his mother continued, undeterred.

"The wealthiest heiress in the county, and one of the wealthiest in the kingdom, I'll wager. Lady Amelia Castleford, wonderful girl, I hear her father recently inherited the Ockington estate. Their coffers must be overflowing." The Marchioness seemed to lick her lips at the thought of all the Castleford gold, but all Hemsbridge could see was the wart on the girl's rather too long nose. Eligible for a more cash-strapped and desperate bachelor than I, he thought, but not for me.

"Mercy me, I fear I shall faint at the sight of all these wonderful young ladies!" said the Marchioness, swaying slightly and trying to keep from broadcasting her insights to the entire room. "Lady Lavinia Witherwood, our host's daughter. Why, isn't she a picture? I shall have to introduce you." Hemsbridge almost let out a most impolite sound as his mother grabbed hold of his arm, pinching it in the process, and led him, rather haughtily, towards Lady Lavinia, where she stood beside her father. As he eyed her, he felt a limited optimism rising within him. The girl was very small for her age it was true, but in the pearly white dress she was wearing, setting off her golden hair, she was rather pretty, in a frail sort of way.

"Your Grace," Hemsbridge's mother said, in the firmer voice she used to communicate with people beyond her immediate family. "May I present my son, the Marquess of Hemsbridge."

"My Lord." Whitehaven said, bowing. He was a tall man with a stern profile, like a general or an especially clever city lawyer. His hair was thinning on top to reveal a rather unsightly red patch, but he had an otherwise distinguished appearance. Hemsbridge duly returned the greeting.

"It is a pleasure to have such esteemed guests in attendance. This is, I fear, only a modest gathering of country society, but my hope is that it shall suffice."

"Oh, certainly my lord, I would not fear, you have assembled such a group of notables as east Somerset has never before witnessed!"

"My Lady is too kind, of course, but immodest as I am, I shall accept your compliment." Hemsbridge, rapidly losing interest in this exchange of formality, was discreetly studying young Lavinia. She returned his glance, and seemed to blush rather girlishly before turning away.

"But where are my manners. May I present my daughter, Lady Lavinia Witherwood." Lady Lavinia turned and curtsied, with a sweet smile that revealed her dimples. "The Marquess of Hemsbridge, and his mother, the Marchioness."

"Charmed" said Hemsbridge casually, bending to kiss Lavinia's hand. She was so frail and retiring that he felt that, if a servant were to open a window, she might be carried away in the ensuing gust of wind.

"My pleasure, Lord Hemsbridge" she just about managed to say. Hemsbridge had to lean forward sharply to make out her words. Her voice was frail and trembling, as if she were lowering herself into a pool of iced water every time she spoke. He noticed her father glance at him expectantly, aiming for the sort of comradely look men often exchange in the presence of attractive ladies. Simultaneously, his mother was nodding at him, far less subtly, to indicate approval. He knew at once that he had no choice but to ask the girl to dance, though he felt little enthusiasm at the prospect.

"Lady Lavinia, it seems the logical choice at this point; would you do me the honour of granting me a dance? That is, of course, if you have any openings on your dance card?" Present company assumed that he was a little stiff in his comment about choice. If only they knew his real opinion, he thought to himself.

"Oh! Oh yes sir, it would be a great pleasure. As it happens, I do have this next dance free."

"Wonderful, then let us proceed." He held out his hand, received another encouraging nod from his mother and his host, and with a wince he just about managed to suppress, took Lady Lavinia's clammy little hand in his and placed it on his arm.

*

As Hemsbridge had very much anticipated, Lavinia Witherwood was not much of a dancer. Her efforts were confounded by a combination of timidity and a waifish, unphysicality that did not lend itself well to this sort of rhythmic exercise. Hemsbridge fancied, from her demeanour, that she was the sort of girl who picked at her food interminably, who preferred green vegetables to a good slab of red meat, did not care for loud music or strong drink and mounted a horse rarely and with great trepidation.

Had he had the time to enquire on any or all of these questions, to one of her intimate associates, he would have discovered that he was correct on all counts and more. She was not, in any sense, a spirited girl.

"Tell me, my Lady" Hemsbridge asked, feigning an interest in his dance partner. "What subjects compel your interest? What accompanies the mind of the Duke of Whitehaven's pretty young daughter?" She blushed uncontrollably at this compliment, tame as it was.

"Why sir, little that would be of much interest to an important gentleman such as yourself. I have a great fondness for needlework, and devote much of my time to its practice. It is but a simple pastime, but it occupies the body and mind as required."

"Scintillating" Hemsbridge managed to squeeze out the words, trying not to roll his eyes. This was at least his third attempt to steer their conversation out of the gentle, shallow waters of chit chat and into the great blue sea of excitement he was seeking, but Lavinia would not oblige.

"I also take bracing walks on the seafront when I can. I find that to be a most invigorating diversion."

"Wonderful. Sea air does one good I suppose?"

"Oh yes sir! It is superb for the constitution!" It took all of Hemsbridge's strength of will to suppress a yawn at this tedious insight. This girl might one day make a fine match for a quiet, timid sort of a chap, he thought, perhaps a vicar, or the underachieving fifth son of some run-of-the-mill minor household. She was not however, the sort of woman who could interest him.

Just as these thoughts were running through his mind, he saw a woman of a very different type, striding boldly across the room.

This was more the sort of woman in whom he could feel an interest! She was tall, with a slender physique, the shape of which could be determined, even in her evening gown. Her slim waist, flaring to well-shaped hips immediately struck him. Her hair, intricately coiffed, sat high upon her head and shimmered golden in the evening's candlelight. She had a certain energy about her, as if the world held little in it that could possibly cause her fear or distress. Gentlemen's heads turned all at once, like willows swaying in unison in the wind, glancing at her, momentarily ignoring the other women in the room. She ghosted through the crush like a wisp, then headed out onto the terrace and was gone. Hemsbridge turned back to his tedious dance partner, who now seemed all the less appealing for being compared to the unknown woman who had just passed through his view.

"You will excuse me, my lady" he said with a slight bow, uncoupling his hands from Lavinia's trembling fingers, as the dance mercifully came to an end. "But I have a pressing need to converse with my valet. A most tawdry affair, but necessary I'm afraid, you will excuse me." The girl whimpered something like "but of course my lord", but Hemsbridge did not tarry long enough to hear it. He moved suddenly with a singular force, slipping across the crowded room, on the trail of that woman who had just caught his eye, interested in no-one and nothing else.

*

Hemsbridge was disappointed to see that the mysterious woman was not, as her earlier course would have suggested, out on the terrace, but was nowhere to be seen.

He scanned his surrounds, trying as hard as he could not to appear odd in front of the other guests, who were enjoying the air on the terrace. He quickly realised that she was definitely not there, was, in fact, not anywhere outside, that he could see.

A middle-aged fellow, with the ruddy look of a man who's indulged in a little too much port, who was outside talking to a girl half his age, turned to him with a look of concern.

"Is everything quite alright, my Lord? You appear to have lost something?"

"I'm fine, thank you, I thought that I had seen someone I know come out here, but it appears I was mistaken." Hemsbridge was muttering, without even turning to make eye contact. "I am now simply taking in some of this fine evening air."

"Got a little stuffy in the ballroom, eh?" the man replied, jokingly, in a tone Hemsbridge did not much care for. "Well I can't say I blame you, there are some handsome ladies in attendance tonight, make no mistake. Why I just saw one of them, slipping through here, popping off with some gentleman friend of hers, out into the gardens. I think I may have some idea of what they had in mind, though it would be neither proper, nor gentlemanly of me to say so, what?!"

The fellow guffawed idiotically, turning Hemsbridge yet further against him. The girl he was with tittered in response to this salacious speculation, but Hemsbridge turned to them. Here was a source of information.

"Did you see where they went?" he asked as calmly as he could, trying to sound as if it was of little import to him.

"Gosh old chap, I don't see it's any of your business is it? Unless she's a lover of yours and you're being made a cuckold, in which case I'm afraid the game is already up!" He punctuated his speak with another raucous laugh, as if this was quite the most amusing idea he had had all evening. "They headed over to those trees yonder, if you must know."

"The trees? And who was the man she was with? What did he look like?" Sterling felt an irrational surge of jealousy, which was very strange, and completely inappropriate – after all, he had only seen the woman once, across a crowded room, and she did not even know that he existed.

"Good grief, I don't know, and I don't quite understand why you care, my good man. But let me think a moment, seeing as you ask. Hmmm…. Yes,… he was sort of tall, dark hair, wearing a red cravat I seem to recall, most unusual."

At this, Hemsbridge's eyes grew wide, and he took a sharp intake of breath. The man he was talking too stepped back, looking a little alarmed at his intensity.

"Was his nose crooked? Positioned oddly to the side like he'd been kicked by a half wild stallion?"

"I only saw him for a second old chap! I wasn't looking out for these sorts of details… though come to mention it, I do believe his nose was rather funny, yes. 'Distinguishing features' I suppose a magistrate might say. This is rather fun actually isn't it, working all this out?"

But Hemsbridge did not reply.

He was staring intently into the distance, over towards the trees, where just this moment, he now knew that the only woman at this ball who could interest him at all was being ravished by a rake, a scoundrel, a bounder, a fellow he had known for many years and with whom he had shared many nights of companionship, and many of sin.

"Aldercott" he muttered at last. "Braydon bloody Aldercott, the bastard."

"I say, do you know this fellow?"

"Of course I know him. I know him rather too well for my liking, or anyone else's for that matter. The swine." Sterling knew that the intensity of his reaction was not rational, that, if he considered it, any woman who would voluntarily go off into the bushes with Aldercott was most likely not very well behaved at all – certainly not a woman whose 'honour' needed defending!

"I say old boy, are you alright?" the man said, abandoning his female companion for a moment, quite distracted by Hemsbridge's intensity.

"You look like you could do with a glass of something stiffer than punch! How about a scotch? I'll have my man fetch you one at once, you look like you've seen a ghost?"

"I haven't. It's quite alright, I'm sure the rascal will skulk back in to explain himself in due course. Farewell." Leaving his companions even more confused than when he had first burst onto the terrace, Hemsbridge returned to the ball.

*

"Do you read scripture at all, Lord Hemsbridge?" said Lady Thrapston, in a shrill tone that made no apologies. The young woman was dowdy and stout, and had planted her arm firmly behind Hemsbridge's back.

"Alas, I find I seldom have the time these days" he replied, giving what he hoped would prove a diplomatic answer.

"No time for the word of God?! Good Lord, what in Heaven or Earth can be the matter with you? I consider any day that does not begin and end on my knees before the heavenly father to be not only wasted, but sinful!"

"An admirable conviction, my Lady."

"Well, I should hope so! Where would we be without the redeeming light of Christ?"

"Where indeed?" Hemsbridge wanted nothing more than to get away, and fast. This was one was far worse than Lavinia Witherwood! The former might have been dull, but at least she wasn't a religious zealot.

"Have you a favourite passage in the Book of Matthew, Lord Hemsbridge?" Lady Thrapston asked, staring at him with what could only be described as fanatical aggression.

"Matthew?" he said, casting about in the back of his mind for some recollection.

He had not read the bible since he was a small boy, and had no especial inclination to start again. Like most energetic young men of the upper-class, religion bored him stiff. "Why, I should have to say Lady Thrapston, I like the entire book too much to possibly select a favoured verse."

"A ridiculous answer, betraying further your impiety!" she snapped back. Bizarrely, her righteous anger was causing her to grip his back more tightly, rather than less. Hemsbridge feared that she had clamped herself to him so hard that he would not be able to flee without employing tactics better kept for a gentleman's wrestling match, something he feared would not go down all that well in polite Somerset society.

"It appears that Somerset is nothing more than a den of godless vipers! If I do not find a good Christian man presently, my return trip to Northamptonshire will have to be brought forward!" and then Hemsbridge was saved. A perfect excuse to leave had just come skulking into the ball room, in the form of his sometime friend and many-time rival Braydon Aldercott.

"You will excuse me my lady..." he said, as politely as he could manage. "Just such a man of virtue and piety has just entered the room, and I am obliged to convey to him my best wishes. You will excuse me." Lady Thrapston looked neither sad nor relieved as he left her, but retained the same expression of anger she had had all along.

"Hemsbridge" said Aldercott as he approached, in the ironic tone of a serial rogue and seducer.

"Aldercott" was all Hemsbridge needed to say in response. They knew each other well enough to dispense with titles, nodding and shaking hands lightly.

"What the devil have you been doing with yourself?"

"I was availing myself of some of the local entertainments," said Aldercott, smirking in his perverse way. "... and by golly were they entertaining."

"Oh yes, indeed?" said Hemsbridge. "Where exactly were you indulging in these 'entertainments'?"

"Why out in the grounds, with the prettiest wee hussy you've ever laid your eyes on. Far better than any of the dogs and dullards you see assembled around this here ballroom." He gestured at the rather boring and unimpressive selection of women Hemsbridge had just now been trying his best to navigate.

"That I can believe. Who was she?"

"Her" said Aldercott, angling his head discreetly in the direction of a woman Hemsbridge immediately recognized. She was the exact same woman who had caught his attention before, and now she seemed even more radiantly beautiful. He noticed that she wore a diamond choker, close and tight about her neck, shimmering along with her pearly earrings and the diamond decorations scattered through her rich blonde hair. He was captivated, but not just by her good looks. It seemed to him that she also had a wryness about her, an awareness of the world and a force for life that was instantly, unconsciously powerful. Compared to the insipid girls he had been forced to speak to, and dance with, she positively shone. This, coupled with the knowledge she had already been engaged in an intimacy that Aldercott, jaded as he was, was willing to describe as 'very entertaining' was enough to get his mind moving rapidly towards the idea of becoming better acquainted with her.

"Lady Amelia Duckington" Aldercott continued. "Married, but you wouldn't know it. Easier and filthier than a barrack room whore. A lot of fellows I know have had their fill of her, Maitland amongst them."

"Maitland fraternized with her?"

Hemsbridge queried, briefly shocked and dragging his eyes away from Lady Duckington for the first time in what felt like hours, but can only have been seconds. Seemingly beyond his control, his eyes drifted back, to follow her progress through the room.

"Oh yes, they were quite a pair for a short while, her matrimonial status notwithstanding. That is, until he decided to run off and marry a serving girl 'for love', or whatever other damn fool excuse he's cooked up since. Duckington over there has been around the block a few times, let me tell you."

"What on Earth can you two fellows be gossiping about?" said Lady Hemsbridge, bustling over to the pair of them in a manner that suggested she had availed herself somewhat enthusiastically of His Grace of Whitehaven's excellent ratafia.

"What is there to discuss, when there are so many fine young ladies here, just waiting for eligible bachelors, such as yourselves, to sweep them off their feet and tuck a wedding ring onto their finger?"

"I dare say, mother, that I have the right to a private conservation with an old friend." Hemsbridge replied, impatient with his mother's insistence on constant attention to the marriage market.

"Pish, and I have the right to butt in, as and when I please, thank you very much! You wouldn't even be here if it wasn't for me."

She declined to mention whether she meant 'at His Grace of Whitehaven's ball' or 'on this earth' by the second remark.

"- and don't tell me you're both smitten with Lady Duckington now?" she continued, following both their eye-lines in the direction of the handsome young adulteress.

"The absurd predictability of men. I ask you! Show them a pretty face and a figure that suits an evening dress and they're off, like hounds after a scent. She may be fair, gentlemen, but she's no lady. A damned hussy if I ever saw one in all my life, and a nasty piece of work to boot."

She delivered this in an indiscreet mangle of words, too angry at the thought of him even looking at Lady Duckington to care who was listening. This, of course, only made Lady Duckington all the more fascinating. Sterling resolved to pursue her acquaintance at the earliest opportunity.

....

Get

"The Marquess' Scandalous Mistress"

as soon as it's released – go to
http://www.ariettarichmond.com

and make sure that you are signed up for news and release
notices !

Books in the 'His Majesty's Hounds' Series

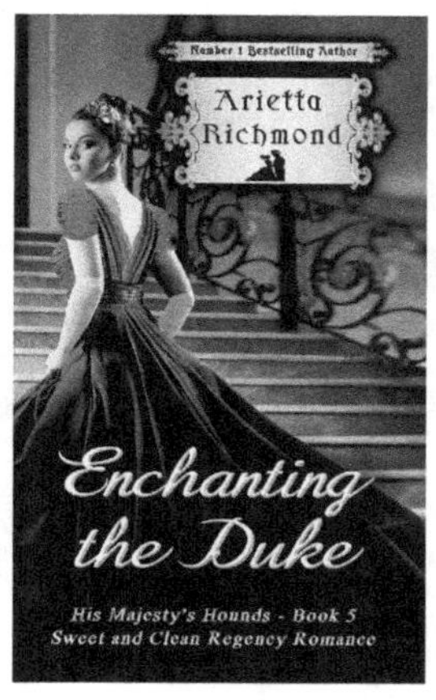

Redeeming the Marquess (coming soon)

Healing Lord Barton (coming soon)

Winning the Merchant Earl (coming soon)

Loving the Bitter Baron (coming soon)

Rescuing the Countess (coming soon)

Attracting the Spymaster (coming soon)

Other Books from Dreamstone Publishing

Dreamstone publishes books in a wide variety of categories – here are some of our other bestselling books:-

We have books in many categories, ranging from Erotica and Romance to Kids Books, Books on Writing, Business Books, Photography, Cook Books, Diaries, Coloring books and much more. New books are released each month.

Be the first to know when our next books are coming out

Be first to get all the news – sign up for our newsletter at

http://www.dreamstonepublishing.com